wedding date for hire

an Anyone But You novel

JENNIFER
SHIRK

Entangled Publishing, LLC
2614 South Timberline Road
Suite 109
Fort Collins, CO 80525
Visit our website at www.entangledpublishing.com.

Bliss is an imprint of Entangled Publishing, LLC. For more information on our titles, visit http://www.entangledpublishing.com/category/bliss

Edited by Stacy Abrams and Lydia Sharp
Cover design by Heather Howland
Cover art from iStock and Shutterstock

Manufactured in the United States of America

First Edition October 2015

Bliss
an Entangled imprint

For Joe and Carolynn:
the two greatest supporters a daughter-in-law could ever ask
for.

Chapter One

It was official. She really was cursed.

After losing her job and her boyfriend, being asked to be maid of honor for two weddings was the final twist of the middle finger her life seemed to be giving her this year.

Maddie McCarthy took a deep breath to steady her anxiety, only to have the seamstress at the Sew What? dress shop take full-on advantage and yank her dress in another inch.

"You, how you say, have a good baby-making hips, yes?" the seamstress said, bobbing her head up and down.

Maddie held in a sigh. Lovely. Now she wasn't going to be able to eat until after the wedding day on top of everything else. Forget the middle finger. Life was giving her the Kim Kardashian special. Thank goodness her mom offered to pay for half of her dress—her savings were meager enough. But if it wasn't for her cheating ex-boyfriend spreading lies about her to the owner, she'd still have her job as head pastry chef at The Ripe Tomato in Boston.

The seamstress gave one final tug then spun her around. Maddie gasped as she took a good hard look at herself in the mirror. She had to admit the charcoal satin gown her sister picked out for her looked pretty darn good against her blond hair. She jumped to the side to inspect herself better. Yep, stomach looked flat, too. No doubt about it. Her sister loved her. The one positive thing going in her life right now.

"Oh, sweetheart," her mom said, walking up to her. "The dress looks beautiful on you." She swatted the seamstress's hands when the woman started to grab more pins. "No. It fits perfectly. You know, Madeline, you could even stand to gain a few pounds."

Maddie rolled her eyes, banking down any and all thoughts of the weight problems she had in high school. She wasn't Fatty Maddie anymore. Thank goodness by the time she'd graduated and gone off to school, she'd grown a few more inches and lost the fifteen pounds of what her mom fondly called "baby fat."

"Thanks, Mom. You look wonderful, too." In fact, her mother looked downright radiant. The best she'd seen her in ages. After years of it being just the three of them—Maddie, her sister, and her mom—one was finally leaving the nest. Louise was getting married. Which would leave Maddie at home with Mom—and, of course, the family curse.

The curtain behind them swung away with a flourish, and Louise stepped out. Maddie's breath caught, and tears began to well in her eyes. Gorgeous. Most people called Louise, who was four years younger than Maddie, a beauty, but dressed in her full bridal gown and veil, she looked absolutely stunning.

Louise wrung her hands. "Well?" she asked, her gaze swinging back and forth between them.

Her mother took a few hesitant steps closer, looking almost afraid to touch her own daughter. "I can't believe my baby will be married in two weeks."

Maddie's heart dropped. Two weeks. Her sister would be starting a new chapter in her life with her new husband. While she was beyond ecstatic for Louise, she still couldn't help wondering…when was it going to be her turn? *If* it would be her turn. The older, wiser, more experienced sister's turn. When would her life come together? So far, she hadn't been able to keep a relationship going for longer than a month. Heck, she couldn't even hold on to a job.

No doubt about it. The curse.

No, no, no. That was silly. Impossible.

Fairly impossible.

She mentally shook herself. "Louise, you are the most beautiful bride I've ever seen in my life."

"Oh, please. I bet you said the same thing to Sabrina when she got married four months ago."

Maddie's best friend, Sabrina, had married Jack Brenner, son of Sabrina's boss at Brenner Capital Investments. Maddie had been the maid of honor in her wedding, too. Sabrina had used Jack in a scheme to make Sabrina's ex-fiancé jealous, but they ended up falling in love with each other for real in the process. As much as she'd wanted to enjoy the day for her friend, Maddie couldn't help feeling a twang of envy, especially since she hadn't even had a date for it. Now it was déjà vu. Only this time she was odd woman out at her own sister's wedding. How pathetic.

Maddie stepped off the platform in front of Louise. "No,

Louise," she said affectionately. "Of course you're the most beautiful bride. You're my sister. We share the same genes."

Louise's lips quirked. "So in essence, you're giving yourself a compliment by complimenting me."

"Naturally."

Their mom chuckled. "Both of you are welcome, then."

Louise group-hugged them. "I love you guys so much." But then she pulled back, gazing at Maddie with concern filling up her blue-green eyes. "I just wish…"

Her sister let the sentence die a natural death. Thank goodness. It was understood. Louise wished Maddie was getting married, too. Or at least had a steady boyfriend. But at this point in her thirty-year-old life, Maddie would settle for a steady job and a place of her own.

"Damn, girl."

Their heads turned in the direction of the feminine voice. Her cousin, Veronica, stood in the doorway of the dress shop with her dark hair pulled back in a bun and her blood-red glossed lips poised in a sassy pout, as if she'd just walked off the set of a Robert Palmer video. "Michael will not make it long past the reception when he sees you in that dress, Louise," she added with a shark-like grin.

Louise gathered up her gown and rushed over to her. "Thank you, thank you," she sang, her voice giddy and happy. "I'm so glad you can make it for all the festivities next week. Michael's parents are really outdoing themselves."

Veronica smirked. "I'll say. But they can afford to."

They sure can, thought Maddie. Louise's fiancé, Michael, came from a very well-to-do family in New England. Although, Michael had made a name for himself and was practically considered royalty in the Boston area, since he was the new franchise owner of the Red Sox. His parents owned a huge estate in Newport, Rhode Island, and planned a week of events there for family and all the bridal party along with their dates. Several guesthouses were on the grounds, so housing would be available for everyone.

Maddie's mom gave Veronica a kiss on the cheek and a light pat on her shoulder.

"Good to see you, Vonnie," Maddie offered.

And by "good to see you" she meant "tolerable to see you." She and her cousin Veronica never really got along when they were young—or now, even. The general air of hostility between them probably had more to do with that giant stick up her cousin's butt than anything else, but it was hard for Maddie to say for sure.

Veronica let her gaze travel the length of Maddie's gown. "Glad you went with that color, cuz. Makes your skin look so much less ashen."

Maddie bit her tongue, choosing to give her a tight smile instead for Louise's sake. The long wedding week ahead just grew about ten times longer.

The seamstress finished writing her notes and stood. "I go and grab other bridesmaid dress from back now."

Veronica held up a hand, stopping the woman in her tracks. "I ordered a black Nicole Miller cocktail dress. Make sure you bring that one out, too." After the woman scurried away, she added to Maddie, "I want to make sure I look my best for the rehearsal dinner. I'm bringing someone I've been seeing for some time now, and I hope to spur wedding ideas of his own."

"Way to think ahead, dear," her mom offered politely.

Veronica's eyes widened. "Aunt Kathy, women in our

family *have* to think ahead, what with the curse and all." She glanced at Maddie, then covered her mouth with her hand. "Oops," she said, not looking the least bit contrite. "But at least *one* of your daughters seems to have broken the curse. Although I suppose anything can happen between now and the wedding."

Louise frowned, and Maddie gritted her teeth. Their cousin should have known better than to mention the curse at a time like this.

The infamous "curse" her cousin referred to—also known as the WD-40 Effect—was a bit of an inside family joke. It was not real. Although, as with all good jokes, of course, there was just a teensy shred of truth to it. The curse was called WD-40 after the lubricant product used to displace moisture and great at removing dirt and residues. The women in Maddie's family seemed to share that specialty, as they were equally as effective in the removal and/or displacement of all men in their life.

Maddie's father disappeared from their lives when Maddie was seven, and her grandfather left when her mom was just in high school. Maddie's great-grandmother and four generations back before then went through the "Effect" as well. She hoped things would be different for her sister and Michael. It seemed to only affect the firstborn women in the family, but Louise still got a little jumpy whenever anyone mentioned the curse, especially with her wedding just weeks away. Veronica's insensitive comments appeared to already have flustered her.

Their mom wrapped an arm around Louise's waist. "Veronica's just kidding about the curse, honey. You and Michael are going to do great."

Veronica batted her eyelashes innocently. "Oh, of course. Not *you*, Louise. I was talking about Maddie here. I mean, she hasn't had a man in her life since the best man dumped her."

Maddie went very still. Then her gaze cut to Louise. "Ryan is the best man?"

Her sister cringed. "I was going to tell you before the wedding. Honest. I just wasn't sure how to break the news."

"Oops again," Veronica said, smothering a smile.

Maddie felt ill. If enduring Veronica's endless jibes about being cursed and having to spend the entire wedding week alone wasn't bad enough, her ex had to be the best man on top of all that.

God, take me now.

Veronica opened her purse to pull out a tube of lip gloss. "Poor Maddie," she said, dabbing more red gloss on her already painted lips. "Looks like the WD-40 Effect lives on."

"That's ridiculous. There's no such thing as a curse," Louise fumed.

Veronica shrugged. "I suppose that's debatable. But it sure seems like there's one in your sister's case."

"There's no curse," Louise insisted. "Maddie has just been under a bit of a dry spell as far as dating goes. Being an old maid doesn't matter to her, anyway."

That did it. Maddie saw red—and it wasn't the goo being globbed on her cousin's lips. She was sick of the jibes. And although Maddie knew her sister meant no malice in her innocently thrown comment, she was sick of the pity, too. Sick of being the one with no job, no man, and no *future*. But most of all, she was sick of hearing about that stupid curse.

"You're all wrong," she blurted. "I do have a boyfriend."

Her sister, mom, and cousin all froze and stared at her.

Oh dear Lord. *Boyfriend? What am I saying?*

But then she remembered Veronica's "poor Maddie" remark and it renewed her resolve. "I—I've been seeing someone for several months now."

"Months?" Louise asked, clearly as shocked as she was.

"Um, yes. I met him right after Sabrina's wedding. He's unbelievably handsome." *Unbelievably handsome?* That remark might have been pushing it. But apparently handsome wasn't all he was because, like her own personal Amtrak line, the words kept coming out of her mouth full steam ahead. "He adores me."

Brain, derail my mouth right now.

"And he's rich," she added.

I mean it, brain! Knock it off.

Her sister threw her arms around her, for which Maddie said a prayer of thanks because it managed to shut her big trap from saying anything further about her adoring, rich, unbelievably handsome—and more importantly *fake*—boyfriend.

"I'm so happy for you," Louise squealed. "But why didn't you tell us?"

Veronica folded her arms. "Yes, Maddie, why didn't you mention him before?"

She gulped. "I didn't mention…" *Good grief, the boyfriend doesn't even have a name.* "I didn't mention *him* before because I didn't want to jinx the relationship and had to make sure he was a keeper. You know because of the whole"—she swallowed—"curse thing."

Her mom kissed her on the cheek. "Well, that's wonderful, dear. I knew you'd find someone in your own time."

"So, dish. How did you meet him?" Louise asked, rubbing her hands together.

She blinked. Good question. *Yes, we had to have met. Somehow…*

"What's his name?" Veronica asked.

She blinked again. His name. *An even better question.*

Maddie's brain scrambled to come up with the answers. But it suddenly felt as if all the oxygen had been sucked out of the room, and her mind couldn't shift out of park. Was it too late to plead mental illness or just plain stupidity? Probably not. Plus, she wasn't sure she'd be able to stand the smug I-told-you-so look on Veronica's face if she admitted she'd lied about being in a relationship.

"I don't want to spoil it. You guys will get to meet him soon enough," she said with a half laugh, half choke.

Louise chuckled. "You're such a tease, Maddie. I think I'm more excited now about meeting your new guy than I am to walk down the aisle."

"Yes," Veronica added, narrowing her eyes. "I look forward to meeting him as well. He must be something for you to keep him under wraps from even your own mom and sister."

Balls of nausea began to take shape in her stomach, but she managed a bright smile. "Yeah, he's something else. Just know that he's great. Really, um, great."

Louise smiled dreamily. "Well, I know he has to be special if you've been seeing him for so long."

A nervous laugh bubbled from her throat. "Oh, he's special." *And nonexistent.*

Maddie turned away, pretending to see a smudge on her dress. If she could have punched herself in the mouth right then and there, she would have. She had completely lost her mind along with everything else she'd lost lately. What the heck was she going to do? She couldn't face her family without a man on her arm. She had to find herself a wedding date now. And not just *any* wedding date. A special-really-something-else-handsome-rich wedding date.

She was doomed.

As if wedding dates like that just hung out at the supermarket checkout line. But if she didn't find one, she'd be the laughingstock of her family. Well, even *more* of a laughingstock. She couldn't bear that.

Her mind raced with potential candidates. And came up with exactly none. She didn't have any handsome or rich male friends she could call. Since she wasn't working, she didn't have any work-related acquaintances she could go to, either. Sabrina's husband Jack tried to set her up with a broker he knew, but that ended up being a complete and utter disaster. She was so screwed!

"Oh, Maddie, look," Louise called to her. "This is how I want the hairdresser to do my hair."

"That is so you," her mom commented.

"Nice," Veronica said. "Very Carrie Underwood-esque."

"What do you think, Maddie? *Maddie*," her sister called again.

Her throat was dry, like someone had stuffed it full of cotton then stuck her out in the sun for a few hours. She finally turned to face them, fighting off hyperventilation. "Y-yes," she croaked. "Of course, let me see."

Louise held out the magazine to her, and she took it from her outstretched hands. The model's hair was pulled back loosely with wispy tendrils and flowers tucked around the bun. Maddie could picture how lovely Louise would look with her long blond hair pulled back in such a style. She was just about to tell her that, but an ad at the corner of the page caught her eye.

Matchmaking/Escort Service

Match Made Easy is for people tired of the struggles of single life. Whether you're looking for a lasting relationship or just a companion for a corporate event or wedding, we'll save you the time and headache. Just answer our simple questionnaire and you'll be assigned your own personal matchmaker. Making your Match is that EASY.

Give us a call or send us an email and start taking control of your love life today!

Maddie blinked. Yes, she could take control of her love life — or rather, have *them* take control of her love life. This was the answer to her big-fat-mouth prayers. An escort service.

"Well?" Louise nudged her with her elbow. "What do you think of the hairstyle?"

"Hairstyle?" She looked at her sister blankly. "Oh, it's very ni— Uh, I mean, I hate it."

Louise and her mother frowned at her.

"What are you talking about?" her cousin asked. "That's the perfect hairdo for Louise."

"Oh, no, she can do better. *Much* better." Then to further prove that point and save the website information, she ripped the page from the magazine and shoved it down her dress.

"Maddie, what on earth is wrong with you?" her sister asked, planting her fists on her hips.

"You mean besides the obvious?" Veronica muttered.

Her mom cocked her head. "Honey, is something wrong? You looked flushed."

Louise made a reach for the article but Maddie jumped back and pressed the paper farther into her bra. "N-nothing is wrong. I just don't want Louise to make a major mistake with her hair. Better to not even be tempted by this dowdy style. It's awful. We'll find another one for you." She pointed her finger toward the seating area. "There are a whole bunch of magazines over there."

Louise continued to stare at her for several long seconds, then finally nodded. "Okay, I guess I do want to find the perfect style." She frowned at Maddie's chest. "However, your methods to express that seem a bit extreme…"

"Let me go change and then we'll get cracking on look-ing for one." Not waiting for an answer, Maddie hurried to the dressing room and, once she was behind the curtain, pulled out the crumpled page from her dress.

Maddie had seen commercials for Match Made Easy on TV. They seemed like a decent business and legit. She hoped. She prayed they weren't out of her price range. Not that it mattered—time was running out. She'd pay anything to prove to her family she wasn't cursed. Plus, Ryan would be there, most likely with that cheating blonde of his. She'd bet anything they'd both love to see her at her lowest point: jobless and dateless. Well, no one was going to feel sorry for her. Not her cousin and certainly not the best man, either.

She'd show them all. And since she couldn't find a wedding date to her sister's wedding on her own, it looked as if she'd be forced to do the next best thing.

Hire one.

"What part of *hell no* do you not understand?"

When his cousin, Kennedy, just stood there gaping at him, Trent Montgomery shook his head in disgust. He didn't have time for her matchmaking shenanigans. He was done helping out. He had his own business to run. From the looks of things this morning, Red Zone Fitness appeared to be a well-oiled machine; however, his gyms were slowly losing money. He needed to figure out why and what to do about it. But first he needed to talk to the spin instructor before her class began. There were some complaints about her music being too loud and it drifting into the yoga room.

He turned away, but Kennedy began to follow him through the gym like a puppy on the scent of bacon. "Trent, please. I wouldn't ask if I wasn't desperate."

Trent stopped to pick up a pair of hand weights somebody left in the middle of the floor, and she ran into his back. "Oof," she muttered.

He turned around as she poked her purple-framed glasses back up her nose, and he had to stifle a grin. His cousin was only twenty-five but her matchmaking/escort business Match Made Easy, which had started out as a simple small business college project, had actually gained momentum and was becoming a viable company. Although, apparently not without a few glitches along the way. Otherwise, she wouldn't be asking him for more help with it.

"Au contraire," he countered, waving a mocking finger in front of her face. "You *would* ask—desperate or not. When you needed financial backing, who did you come to? Me. When you needed website help, who did you come to? Me again. And when you needed—"

"Fine," she huffed. She flung her hands up in the air. "It's established that I ask you for a lot of things, but it just so happens that I really am desperate now. I need you. So *pleeeeeease* help me out here. I'm begging."

Trent glanced around his gym, and when he saw that the spin class had already started, he sighed, staring down at her. "Okay. What kind of help are we talking about here?"

"I need you for a simple escort job. That's all."

Trent wasn't born yesterday. He knew how to read the fine print in any contract and also when to decipher his cousin's definition of the word "simple."

"And just how long is this so called simple job?" he asked. She bit her lip. "Oh, that. Well…"

"Kennedy," he warned. "How long is this simple job? Two hours? Three?"

"Four and a half days," she coughed out through her hand.

He blinked. "Four and a half…*days*? That's essentially five days. Are you *insane*?"

"I know it's a bit of a commitment. But Trent, please. The family of the groom is hosting a ton of parties for this wedding and—"

"Wedding?" He glared at his cousin. "That makes it a double *hell no* and you know it."

Everybody—especially Kennedy—knew he did not do

weddings. Ever. He avoided them at all costs, along with cheap beer, Barbara Streisand music, yogurt, and any movie that had characters dressed up in Jane Austen time period garb. He shuddered.

"Sorry. No can do, kiddo. Weddings are a deal breaker. You're going to have to find yourself some other escort fill-in. I'm out this time."

"But—but I already tried, and I need someone extremely good-looking."

He smirked. "Nice try."

"Not only that. Someone smart and"—she fluttered her fingers around his chest and shoulders—"*fit*. This woman needs more than a simple escort. It's her sister's wedding, and family weddings are special. She can't bring just anyone. She has to have someone who her family will believe is actually her boyfriend. And what mother wouldn't love to have you date her daughter?"

He folded his arms, trying not to be amused. "Again, I'll give you major suck-up points, but my answer is still no. Besides, why on earth would you take a job like that if you couldn't fulfill it?"

Kennedy's chin shot up. "Hey, I absolutely could fill it. I'm a professional here. Laird was all set and perfect for the job until the, uh, incident."

"Incident?"

"Yeah. Toaster incident." She wrinkled her nose. "Apparently, he and his girlfriend had a bad breakup over the weekend. Now that I think about it, I probably should send flowers. He's still in the hospital. Laird suffered second degree burns"—with pink flushed cheeks, her gaze traveled past his belt buckle then bounced back up again—"in the frank and beans area, if you know what I mean."

Trent winced. *That must have been one hell of a break-up*. "Don't you have a backup guy for these kinds of... *emergencies*?"

"Unfortunately, no. Not yet. It takes time to build up an escort base as well as a client base. There are two conventions going on in Boston within the next few days and a number of women who wanted someone to accompany them to various cocktail parties. I'm already using everyone I have. Besides, this client was pretty specific in her escort request. Laird was the closest man I had who fit her criteria. So, now we're stuck."

Trent lifted an eyebrow. "Correction. *You're* stuck."

"No, I mean *we*. You're invested in this business just as much as I am. Normally, I would refund her the money, but this gig could be huge for me — *us*. The wedding is a very big deal. The bride is marrying Michael Lyons. That's a foot in the door to advertise in Fenway Park. Plus, you have no idea how many celebrities and potential upscale clientele we could gain from this if she's happy with Match Made Easy. It'll look great to investors, too. And if business really starts to take off from it, well, the sooner you'll have your money back that you need to renovate your gyms and pay off your business loan."

"I don't know..."

"I'll be able to give you back your money with interest, and then you'll have enough for that program you want to start here in the gym."

The mention of his youth group idea suddenly had his attention. Ever since he graduated college and opened his fitness center, he had visions of starting up a after school program in his home town of Midship, MA. He wanted it for high school athletes who needed more than just physical training. He wanted a program in his gym that went deeper. That could serve as a kind of character coach for these young men. A place they could go for support if there was no family support. Something he could have desperately used himself when he'd been growing up.

Now he needed the money for updated equipment and to pay off his line of credit, which was coming due soon. Trent had the funds for it all a few years ago, but then his cousin came to him when she needed financial backing for her matchmaking business, and he'd given it to her. How could he not? Kennedy was the only person who stuck by him after he had suffered his football-career-ending injury in college. His own fiancée hadn't even stood by him. That was when he found out who his true friends were.

And that he hadn't had many of them.

Kennedy grabbed his arm and gave a little squeeze. "Trent, women love you and you know it. I don't want to fink out on this woman. What if she reports me to ADAMS?"

"Who's that?"

"Not who. What. ADAMS is the Association of Dating Agencies and Matchmakers. I don't want a black mark against my name there. I've worked too hard, and I have a reputation to uphold. Plus, I don't know, I kind of liked her. She seems really...really..."

"Nice?" he finished for her.

She shook her head. "Desperate. I want to help her."

Desperate.

He rolled his eyes. That was the third nail in the coffin to this whole fiasco. Kennedy wanted him to pose as a paid escort (which embarrassed him) to a desperate woman (which scared him) and take her to a wedding (which nauseated him).

Oh, yeah, he liked that idea.

Trent closed his eyes as if that would help draw the strength he needed not to put his cousin in a headlock. He drew in a breath and, when he opened them again, he found her gazing up at him with big brown hopeful eyes. The word "sucker" reflected back in them, and she grinned as if she knew what his answer would be before he even opened his mouth.

Hell. Of course he would say yes. He didn't have the heart to let her down. Plus, as much as he hated the idea of posing as arm candy for some strange woman, he had a lot riding on the success of Kennedy's business, too.

"What's this woman's name?" he grumbled.

Kennedy squealed, jumping up and down, then threw her arms around his neck. "You are the best cousin ever," she said, giving him a loud kiss on the cheek. "Her name is Madeline McCarthy. She's about your age. Maybe a year or two younger. You'll like her. She has a great personality."

Trent tried not to make a face, but when Kennedy said "great personality" that usually translated to "boring" and quite possibly "allergic to working out." But the name sounded vaguely familiar. Then again, when he was the star college quarterback for the Florida Fireballs, he'd attracted more women than a David's Bridal wedding dress sale. He'd bet he'd probably met a hundred Madelines back then—when everybody loved him and thought he was some kind of freakin' football god. Including his own fiancée. Then that bubble burst along with his future career. He'd eventually gotten over both. He'd become the successful business owner to three Red Zone Fitness Centers in the North Shore area of Massachusetts, and he now just enjoyed female companionship for what it was truly worth. A temporary means to an end. A *fun* and temporary means, but it all still led to an end—one that he always made sure to initiate.

No harm, no foul that way.

Kennedy reached out and gave his cheek an affectionate pat. "Hey, I'm sorry that it has to be a wedding. But maybe it'll be good for you. You know, a hair-of-the-dog kind of thing," she added with a wobbly smile.

Hair of the dog. Huh. If that were the case, he was about to choke down one supersized Bernese mountain dog kind of milkshake over the next few weeks. But if it was good for Kennedy's business, it would mean the extra money he sorely needed, so he'd grin and dazzle this woman until her head spun. And pray it was the last time he'd ever have to help out with the "family business" again.

"I'm a big boy, Ken. I can handle a wedding event." He hoped. "So when do I meet this desperate woman with the great personality?"

"I'm glad you asked." His cousin suddenly dropped her hands, clearing her throat as if she had a wad of cotton lodged in it. "Now, don't get huffy," she began.

Trent frowned at her. "Huffy? You are not allowed to refer to me or any man as huffy. In fact, you telling me not to get huffy is getting me…well, huffy."

Kennedy checked her watch. "Okay. Then don't get upset with me, because I figured you would agree to play escort for me. Eventually." She glanced over his shoulder then swallowed again. "It's just that, well, your future wedding date just walked in."

Chapter Two

Between lying to her family and hiring an escort service to save face, Maddie figured her life at this point had all the makings of an award-winning reality TV show.

Thank goodness she really liked and trusted the owner of Match Made Easy, Kennedy Pepperdine. Maddie needed someone like her in her corner. Kennedy was about her age and seemed professional and completely empathized with Maddie's dateless plight. She assured her that she had her very best man lined up for the job—which was a huge relief. Maddie needed nothing less than a 100 percent perfect man, otherwise she wasn't sure she'd be able to pull off this fake wedding date fiasco.

She was about to invest a good chunk of her savings on this ploy, so it had to go right. But it would be worth it to squash the family curse rumor for a while and to have her ex—Ryan—see that she'd found somebody else so quickly, especially since he was the one who had caused her to lose her job in the first place. The rat.

Her eyes burned from lack of sleep as she gazed around the gym. Maddie considered Red Zone Fitness as the meeting place a bit odd, but Kennedy assured her that neutral everyday atmospheres worked best for first meets. So here she was, looking out of place—and now that she thought about it, a little out of shape. She adjusted her running shorts, which seemed a bit tighter than usual. She could feel them inching up her butt cheek with the slightest of movements. What made her think she could meet her date, then squeeze in a workout?

It was Maddie's first time there, but she liked what she saw of the gym. The workout area had a good mix of men and women of all ages. The treadmills faced the windows, which overlooked part of Massachusetts Bay, but had tinted glass so people walking along the paved path couldn't see in. Despite needing a little TLC, everything looked clean and neat. She could see herself working out here. Maybe, if she enjoyed working out. Or if she ever just…worked out.

Maddie checked her cell phone for the tenth time for any missed messages from Kennedy. *Where is she?* Maddie felt so desperate and shady, waiting to meet her hired "date." Everyone who looked at her seemed to know exactly why she was here, like she had a giant *L* on her forehead. Ugh. She closed her eyes and prayed for the ground to open and swallow her whole. Then, when that didn't happen, she prayed for looser shorts.

"Maddie!"

Her eyes sprung open when she heard her name called out from across the room. Kennedy bounced on her heels and waved her over from across the room. *Finally!* She pulled on her gym shorts one last time before heading over, but dread froze her feet to the ground when she noticed the man standing next to Kennedy.

Oh, crappity-crap-crap. She could never forget a face like that. Trent "Money" Montgomery. *Please, let there be some mistake.*

But then Kennedy whispered something in his ear, and he nodded. Oh, no. Before she could contemplate turning around and hightailing it out of there, Trent's gray gaze caught hers and held for several long seconds before he offered her up one of those dazzling smiles she remembered him using on all the high school cheerleaders years ago.

Mama. And just like that, her traitorous knees did an odd little wobble.

Trent had been given the nickname "Money" in high school, because he was known for throwing passes that were right on the money. That name had followed him throughout his college career, too. Then he suffered an injury that ended his would-be NFL career. It was all anyone from town talked about when the accident had happened. Not that she paid any attention to college football talk. Or Trent Montgomery. At least not anymore.

That was a lifetime ago.

Physically, Trent hadn't changed a bit—probably because of some deal he'd made with the devil or most likely because he *was* the devil. He was striking and sexy, in a cavalier jock kind of attractiveness. Football had given him all those ridiculous muscles, and even though he probably hadn't played the game in years, he hadn't lost one single ounce of that perfect athlete's body.

Not that she was ogling him or anything. Not at all. In

fact, if he'd worn a T-shirt that actually fit him instead of a size smaller than he was, she would have missed his Popeye-sized biceps entirely.

He didn't even look like he remembered her. Well, two could play that game. It was just as well. She had harbored a secret crush on him back in high school until she realized what a complete and total jerk he was.

Yeah, Trent Montgomery as her wedding date for a whole five days was not going to work. *Anyone* but him. She wouldn't be caught dead hiring someone like Trent—a guy who completely embarrassed her in high school.

Kennedy rushed over to her. "Maddie, you're right on time," she said, holding out a delicate ivory hand.

Maddie numbly shook it, glancing around the gym one last time to make sure there weren't any other tall, handsome men Kennedy could have possibly brought with her to be her wedding date. No such luck. Although, considering the alternative, the senior citizen with the droopy sweatpants in the corner had some potential.

Kennedy's mouth stretched into a wide, beaming smile. "I want to say that I personally looked over your questionnaire and, with great care that you can only get at Match Made Easy, have come up with the perfect escort for your sister's wedding. In fact, I was just about to brief Trent but since you're here, I'll introduce you two, and you can get to know each other on your own."

Maddie frowned. Funny, but she thought escorts would use a stage name for their clients. Less chance of inviting stalkers or women who wanted to call on them for any *off-duty* services. She stepped closer to Kennedy, avoiding eye contact with Trent and his biceps, and cleared her throat.

"Uh, can I have a word with you?"

Kennedy bobbed her head up and down, sending her dangly earrings swaying like porch swings during a hurricane. "Of course. But first, I want you to meet Trent. You're going to have to agree that he meets all the criteria you've listed."

Maddie finally allowed her gaze to travel over to Trent. *Lordy*. He certainly did meet all the criteria she listed. And then some. On a scale of one to ten in the looks department, Trent scored a "twelve—too hot for mere mortal eyes." Unfortunately, Maddie learned the hard way that looks couldn't make up for personality. There was no way she was going to pay good money for his company. She'd much rather face humiliation from her family.

"A pleasure," he said in a smooth, deep voice.

No, it most certainly was not a pleasure. It was a mistake. A huge and disappointing I-better-get-my-deposit-back mistake.

Kennedy clasped her hands expectantly. "Well? What do you think?"

Think? No thinking about it. She cleared her throat, turning her head ever so slightly so Trent wouldn't hear her, and whispered, "I think I'd like a refund."

*R*efund?

Trent didn't shock easily, but for the first time in his life he was left speechless. This woman was actually turning him down as her wedding date?

His cousin seemed confused too and turned three shades of pink before eventually settling on a pale puke green. "W-what do you mean?" she asked. "The wedding wasn't canceled, was it?"

The woman named Maddie gave him another nervous glance before addressing Kennedy again. "Uh, no." She leaned in and lowered her voice again. "It's just that I don't want"—she tried to point in a subtle manner, but it was hard for him not to notice, considering she was less than a foot away—"*him.*"

Trent's brows shot up. He tugged on the collar of his T-shirt and took a quick sniff of himself. When that checked out, he ran his hand over his mouth and cheeks to make sure no remnants of his breakfast were hanging off. All clear on that front, too.

Huh. Well, this was a first. He considered himself one of those eligible-dating-material kind of guys. Women certainly seemed to think so. *Other* women, anyway. He never had problems getting dates. He was even voted Best Looking in high school.

So what the hell is her problem anyway?

Kennedy's eyes widened as she glanced at him. "I'm sorry. I'm a little confused. What's wrong with Trent? He's gorgeous," she said in a family pride sort of manner.

Maddie turned her back on him. "That may be the case, but I'm still going to need some sort of do-over."

"Do-over?" His cousin shook her head. "I—I can't do a do-over. Not on this short notice."

"Well, I'm afraid I'm going to need a refund then."

That did it. Trent had heard enough and was tired of standing by like a piece of auctioned meat. And *unwanted* auctioned meat at that.

"Excuse me." He tapped the blonde none too lightly on her shoulder. When she turned around, surprise froze the curt words that teetered on the tip of his tongue.

Well, hell. The woman was even prettier than he originally thought. Satiny blond hair brushed her shoulders with just enough bounce and curl that made him want to reach out and touch a strand. She had a nice body, too—not necessarily athletic, but trim and soft in all the right places. The frown she aimed at him only accentuated her full bottom lip that was shiny from gloss or maybe from nervously licking it.

Why in the world does this woman need to hire an escort service?

Cool blue eyes stared back at him. "I'm sorry, but this doesn't concern you."

She was about to turn away again, but he placed a gentle hand on her arm. Her muscles tensed, but for some reason he didn't let go. "Actually, it does concern me," he told her. In more ways than she would ever realize. He had a stake in his cousin's business and, as much as he hated the idea of posing as a wedding date, he couldn't afford to let Kennedy or the company down.

Kennedy held her hands up, making the time-out sign. "Okay, okay. We all have to take a deep breath here. I think a change of scenery is in order. All this spandex obviously has everyone on edge."

"No," Maddie said firmly, removing his hand from her arm. "If you don't have anyone else, then this isn't going to work. I'm sorry, Kennedy, there isn't anything else to discuss." And with that, she skirted by both of them and began speed walking down the row of elliptical machines with two clenched fists at her side.

Trent blinked at the woman's retreating back then shamelessly allowed his gaze to drift down to her sashaying hips.

Kennedy grabbed his arm, righting his gaze again. "What in the world did you say to her?"

"What? Hmm…let's see, I smiled and said, 'A pleasure.' Yep, that must have been it. I probably should have used a complete sentence and said, 'A pleasure *to meet you.*' Somebody call the grammar police!"

She snorted. "There has to be more to it than that."

"The woman obviously has issues, too."

"Well, we can't let her walk out like that. Something is wrong."

"Yeah, like she's mental."

"Trent," she scolded, "this is serious. You have to go after her and smooth things out."

"*Me?* Why me? You're the CEO. I thought I was just being billed as 'the pretty face' in this partnership."

"Look, she was all set to sign on the dotted line until she saw you. This account is important to the investors and me. It should be important to you, too. Please, Trent, for the company. For *your* company. Go after her," she said, giving him a slight push in that direction. "Time is wasting. She's probably halfway to Maine by now."

Remorse twisted his insides. Kennedy was right. Maddie might be a fruit loop, but he needed the money. "Fine." He sighed, then he took off in her direction.

Fortunately, he found her five seconds later. The woman wasn't anywhere near halfway to Maine, but by all accounts, she was about halfway from an embarrassing 911 call.

"What do you think you're doing?" he barked, coming up behind her.

Maddie—whose forearm was wedged up one of his

vending machine drop slots—lifted her pert nose at him as if she were royalty and he a common serf. "I'm retrieving my Diet Coke, thank you very much."

He smothered a grin. "Well, before you can *retrieve* your soda, you must first insert your money."

She huffed out an exaggerated breath. "I understand that, Captain Obvious, and I already did. This stupid machine moved the can just close enough not to fall. It's probably the owner's way of getting extra money."

He bit down on his tongue at that remark, considering he *was* the owner.

Maddie shoved her arm farther up the slot. "I almost have it."

"Will you take your arm out of there before we have to saw it off?"

Fire sprung in those blue eyes of hers, making her look even more adorable, he decided. Like angry Tinker Bell. "Don't tell me what to do."

Trent gazed heavenward. Great. Not only would he have to place that 911 call when her arm got stuck, but then he'd probably have to call his attorney, too, for when she sued him. It wasn't such a wonder anymore why she needed help getting that wedding date. This woman was trouble with a capital *T*.

Trying a different tactic, he gently placed a hand on her shoulder and leaned in. "You're right. It's none of my business. Stay in that position all day if you want. The guy on treadmill number two is getting quite the view. One more deep squat and I guarantee he'll be asking for your number."

"What?" Cheeks on fire, she sprung up. She glanced behind her then turned toward him with narrowed eyes.

"Hey, that was a dirty trick. There's no guy over there."

"No, but if there were he would have been treated to a dazzling display of hot pink thong. Not to mention that I'm sure my 'dirty trick' just saved you at least eight weeks of physical therapy. And by the way, you're welcome."

Maddie folded her arms, but there was a hint of a smile on those luscious lips of hers. "For the record, it's not hot pink. It's neon crystal pink. But thanks," she muttered.

Trent sighed then nodded. "How about we start over? I'm Trent Montgomery." He stuck out his hand to her.

She glanced at it, not bothering to shake it, and immediately lost her smile. "I know who you are, Trent. We went through four years of high school together."

He squinted at her. *Four years?* Impossible. There was no way he would have gone all through his high school years without noticing or asking her out at least once. "Are you sure?"

"I'm sure." Her expression became a mask of impassive coolness. "As sure as you asking me to your junior prom."

He blinked. "We went to the junior prom together?" *What the hell? It's getting worse.*

"No. I said you *asked* me to your junior prom. Then two weeks before, one of your jock buddies told me it was some sort of varsity hazing ritual to ask someone out from marching band. Some joke. I had bought a dress and everything."

Okay, not getting worse. It was worse. Then a memory popped into his mind. "Wait. You're *Fatty Maddie*?"

Her chin shot up, and she pinned him with a kind of disdain reserved only for delinquent dads or men who kicked puppies. "It's just Maddie nowadays, but yes," she said in a frosty tone.

He winced. Of all the women he would need to depend on for his business, it was dumb luck that it would turn out to be a girl his buddies practically tortured in school. A dull throb filled his temples, and he reached up both hands to massage them.

He should have been more surprised at his actions, but it wasn't hard to picture himself going along with something like that back then. When his buddies had teased Maddie about her weight, he had said nothing. Never came to her defense. But he had been a rotten teenager, constantly looking for approval and acceptance from his friends since his parents were never around to give him those things. It was one of the reasons he wanted to start a youth program in his gym for high school boys. To make a difference but to also keep young men from becoming what he had been: a self-absorbed ass.

"I'm sorry," he told her, finally dropping his arms. "I didn't exactly hang around with the best crowd back then."

Maddie shrugged. "Water under the bridge. We're both mature adults now. Well, *I* am, at least."

"So you not wanting to hire me has nothing to do with our so-called past? I mean, since you're the mature adult in this equation here."

"That's right. It has absolutely nothing to do with high school." But the waver in her voice combined with the way she didn't meet his eyes when she answered told him a different story—like this woman knew how to hold a grudge.

Not that he blamed her. He could tell he had hurt her back then. And for that, he felt like a true jackass. No wonder the woman didn't want to hire him as her date. She probably didn't even want to be in his presence now. But he had to change her mind.

"I find that hard to believe." He stepped closer to her and caught a pleasing scent of citrus mixed with flowers—like springtime and sass in a bottle. He barely knew this woman, but somehow the fragrance suited her. Everything about her seemed fresh and clean and bright. All the way from her neon pink panties to the robin's-egg blue color on her fingertips. He wondered how he'd missed someone so vibrant all those years ago even in just passing.

Then he frowned, suddenly remembering the real reason he had gone after her in the first place: so she'd reconsider and use his cousin's escort service. Which actually was turning out to be a more interesting job than he originally thought.

"Look, I'm perfectly fine," she told him in a no-nonsense tone. "So get over yourself. We were both kids. As you can see, I'm unaffected by what you did back then."

As a beautiful woman in desperate need of a hired wedding date, he had to assume she was affected by *something*. Not that her problem was his to solve. He had enough of his own, including getting his investment money back from his cousin's business.

He cleared his throat. "I'm glad to hear it. I guess I'm hired then."

Hired. Ugh. The word still sounded bizarre. He couldn't believe he was one step away from actually begging. But if Maddie asked, he wouldn't be averse to dropping down on his knees and doing just that.

She scoffed. "I don't think so. It's kind of awkward at this point, you pretending to be my date and all."

"One little mishap in high school doesn't have to be

awkward."

She pursed her lips, staring him down. "Did you know you also broke my glasses on senior prank day?"

Oh, crap. He sighed then shook his head.

"Well, you did. You and your buddies bought hundreds of those super bouncy balls and dropped them from the second floor onto underclassmen below, one of whom happened to be me. One bounced right in my face and knocked off my glasses, then a girl in a wheelchair ran over them while she was trying to roll out of the way. My mom made me spend my own money to buy a new pair."

He rubbed his face with his hand and prayed he hadn't done anything else to this woman. Karma certainly was a bitch, or in his instance, a five-foot-five blond pixie who wore contacts and had an elephant memory. "Uh, sorry about that, too, then."

She blew her hair out of her face, sending curls dancing along her cheek. "Look, Trent, no offense, but this whole situation combined with our pasts is just a little…weird. It won't work. I'm not that good of an actress to pretend that I like you, let alone that I'm smitten with you. And right now, I literally can't afford for anyone not to believe me."

"You don't need to worry about that. Leave it to the professionals at Match Made Easy."

Maddie cocked an eyebrow. "The professionals. You mean *you*?"

"Yes, uh, me." *Sort of.* Maybe he wasn't exactly an escort professional. But he knew women well enough. How hard could this job be anyway? All he had to do was think of it as a one hundred and twenty hour date…

Kennedy better be right about this job being good for

business.

"My sister was four years behind us in school. Do you really think for one second she is going to fall for any of your lines? She knows what you did to me."

"Okay, I can see where there might be some issues for you, but I can guarantee you that I've changed." He *had* changed. He made a show out of crossing his heart to help prove his case. "Maddie, you're going to have to trust me on this."

"Ha! I don't trust you as far as I can—"

"Maddie!" a female voice called.

"What now," she said with a groan.

They both turned in the direction of the voice. A very attractive brunette walked over to them, all smiles and white teeth for Maddie. "Hey, Maddie," she said once she stood next to them. "What are you doing here? I thought you said you were allergic to working out."

Trent held in a grin but glanced over at Maddie with raised eyebrows.

Maddie's cheeks colored. "Uh, no, Sabrina. I said I have *allergies* and quite possibly"—she fake-coughed several times—"exercise-induced asthma. That's why I don't work out. I prefer good old-fashioned walking," she said, pumping her arms back and forth.

Sabrina's brows furrowed. "Then what are you doing here?"

"I…was just passing through…on my walk."

"Passing through a gym?" Sabrina chuckled. "I don't think so. I know you too well. Not unless there was a Krispy Kreme on the other side of it. Does this have anything to do with your friend here?" she said, giving her a knowing smile.

Maddie blinked. "Friend? Who?" She glanced at Trent in horror. "NO! Not at all. He's not a friend, he's—"

"Her boyfriend," Trent blurted. This was it. This was his one chance to seal the deal, and he was grabbing it. He then threw his arm around Maddie and pulled her into his chest.

"He's not my boyfriend," Maddie mumbled into his T-shirt.

Sabrina raised questioning eyebrows at him. "Are you or aren't you?"

He gritted his teeth but smiled. It was obvious Maddie wasn't going to take a knee and make this easy for him. "Maddie has a wonderful sense of humor. It's one of the things I love about her."

Maddie managed to wriggle out of his embrace, shooting him such a sharp look that he almost checked for blood.

"So nice to finally meet you, Sabrina," he went on to say. "I've heard so much."

Sabrina looked at him blankly. "Really? That's funny because I've heard absolutely nothing about you." Then her eyes widened at Maddie, and she smacked herself on the forehead. "Oh, I get it. You didn't mention him to me because you didn't want to jinx it, right? I knew you believed in the family curse. Well, I wouldn't have told me, either. I've read curses—and voodoo hexes—can be very tricky to eliminate."

Maddie gulped and looked at a loss for words. Sabrina mentioning a family curse threw him for a loop, too. Fortunately for Maddie, in his lifetime, he'd picked up his share of fumbles, so he was prepared to pick up hers and run all the way to the end zone with it. "You are so correct," he said smoothly. "We've been keeping it a secret for exactly that reason. But then again, ever since I met Maddie, I haven't wanted to let her out of my sight for one minute."

Sabrina looked to Maddie. "Is that why you haven't called lately?"

"I—"

"We've been pretty...*busy*," he added with a wink.

Sabrina chuckled. "Ah. Well, all is forgiven then." She glanced at the time and frowned. "I'd love to hear more about how you two met, but I don't want to miss my yoga class. We can catch up at Louise's wedding."

Maddie finally found her voice. "Y-yes, we'll talk more at the wedding."

Sabrina cocked her head at Trent. "I guess I'll be seeing you there, too?"

Trent nodded emphatically. "You bet. Wouldn't miss attending Maddie's sister's wedding for anything. Curse or no curse. Isn't that right, *honey*?"

When Maddie kept her jaw clenched, he gave her shoulders a subtle little shake. She caught on fast and looked up at him with an ultra-bright Miss America smile. "That's right, schnookie," she said to him through her teeth.

Sabrina beamed at both of them. "Great. And Maddie, don't even think about the curse now. In fact, I promise not to mention it again, either. I'm just so glad you've met someone and can prove to your family that the curse is finally broken." With a little wave, she then took off in the direction of the yoga room.

Trent turned to her with a frown. "What's this about a curse?"

Maddie ignored his question, planting both fists on her hips. "What do you think you're doing?"

"Helping you."

"You mean helping yourself," she spat.

"No, I mean helping *you*. Maddie, listen. You don't seem like the kind of woman who would call Match Made Easy on some whim. There must have been a pretty darn good reason. Or maybe even more than one. Start being honest with yourself, and don't let your pride about what happened in our past get in the way. I can help you with whatever that reason is in the present. If you let me."

Maddie looked down at her hands, wrung together in one giant knot of tension. He was right. This woman didn't just want simple company at this wedding. There was definitely more to it. But he had to remind himself that whatever the reason was, it wasn't his concern.

After several long moments, she finally conceded. "Okay," she breathed. "Fine. I really don't have a choice at this point. You're hired."

Yes! He couldn't wait to tell his cousin. Luckily for his self-respect, he had seen the end zone before and was able to school his expression into a perfect mask of impassiveness.

"Great," he said. "Let's go talk to Kennedy then." He started in that direction but after several steps, realized Maddie wasn't following.

When he glanced back, he saw Maddie no longer wore the troubled expression of a defeated woman desperate for a date. Instead, she'd taken on a warrior stance with those glossed lips of hers settled into a fine tight line. "Look, hot shot, Sabrina may think that we're a couple, but my family can spot bad acting faster than Roger Ebert at a B-movie festival, so you better be convincing."

He advanced another step and had the satisfaction of

seeing her lose a little of that tough-act bravado. "I can be very convincing," he assured her in a voice several octaves deeper than he intended.

"Well…all right then." She bit her lip. "I'm paying a lot for you so I don't want there to be any mistakes."

Trent managed to drag his eyes away from that shiny mouth of hers and grinned. "Don't worry, sweetheart. I guarantee I'll be worth every penny."

Chapter Three

Trent Montgomery better be worth every penny.

With a queasy feeling, Maddie signed the check with the first half of her payment to Match Made Easy and stuffed it in an envelope.

A male escort as her wedding date. Ugh. Her life had hit an all-time low.

She sank her head into her hands—a tame action, considering she really wanted to stuff her head into the toilet and flush. Was it truly that important to attend her sister's wedding with a gorgeous guy on her arm and show her mom, her cousin, that dirtbag of a best man, and the rest of her family that she was not a loser and not in fact cursed?

Yes. Yes, unfortunately, it was.

She would have spent almost any amount of money, too. Money she didn't really have just to stop the talk and whispers, even if only temporarily. She had to dip into her dismal savings she had hoped would last until she found another job. Not that she faulted her family. They didn't understand the pain she'd feel whenever she heard the jokes start to crack.

Looks like our dear Maddie gave another man the slip.

Hey, Maddie, have you bought stock in WD-40 yet?

Poor Maddie still hasn't found a job. The curse hasn't stopped at her love life.

Maddie took several deep breaths until she was strong enough to raise her head again. Everything was going to be fine. Her life would get better. It would. She had to believe that. She just needed to get through her sister's wedding first.

A knock at her door sounded, then her mom stuck her head in. "All clear? Hi, sweetie."

Maddie rolled her eyes. "Mom, please. This is your house, and I'm thirty years old. I'm hardly sneaking boys up to my room at this stage of my life."

"Maybe not boys, but perhaps *one* man in particular," she teased, having a seat on her bed. "So why don't you tell me about him."

"About who?"

"That's what I'd like to know," she said with a chuckle. "I don't even know your boyfriend's name."

"Boyfriend?" She blinked. "Oh, right. *Boyfriend.*" She smacked her hand against her forehead. Gosh, it would be good if she remembered that small tidbit if she wanted to make this wedding date work. "Yes, his name is Trent. Trent Montgomery."

Her mom's brows furrowed in thought. "Didn't you go to school with a Trent Montgomery? He was a football player and very cute if I recall."

Maddie sent her a weak smile. Leave it to her mom to

remember those details of her high school experience. "Uh, yeah. That's him all right." Although if she were being honest, she'd hardly describe Trent as "cute." Adonis, stud-like, hottie McHot-Hot, even pulchritudinous—all acceptable descriptions. Hardly just cute.

Her mom frowned. "Wasn't he the one who—?"

"Yes." She cleared her throat, trying to block out all the embarrassing high school experiences. "Yes, that Trent Montgomery. But it's all in the past. Apparently he's very nice now."

"Apparently?"

"I mean, he *is* nice now. Of course he is. Um, he's great." She managed to hold in a snort. Trent hardly seemed nice or great or changed at all. What kind of conceited man capitalizes on his good looks and becomes a male escort anyway? He was practically one step away from being a gigolo. Good grief. Maybe it was a mistake to hire him for her only sister's wedding after all.

Her mom cocked her head. "Honey, are you okay? You look a little…green."

"Uh, it's probably the stress of the wedding that has me a little wiped. How's Louise holding up?" she said, anxious to change the subject.

"She and Michael are in Newport already. I imagine his parents are trying to take care of a lot of the wedding details for her. She mentioned Michael even scheduled a spa appointment to help her relax."

Maddie smiled. Her sister had found a gem of a guy. "Michael is so good for her. I hope they last."

"Maddie! Of course they'll last. Why on earth would you think otherwise? Are you letting what Veronica said the other day get to you?"

She made a face. "I try not to let *anything* Veronica says or does get to me."

But in truth what her cousin had said about the curse had gotten to her. If she wasn't cursed, why couldn't she keep a man interested? She'd never been able to get to know a guy long enough to ever fall in love. Even her own father—the man she'd worshipped and had thought felt the same about her—didn't think she was worthy enough to stick around for. They had been so close, too. He'd read to her almost every night when she was a child, just the two of them. He'd sneak in her favorite chocolate mints, and she'd slowly savor each bite as he read, basking in the attention he'd given to her. Those were the best days. Then one day he was gone. No good-bye. No note.

Nothing.

It had pretty much set the tone for the way men fizzled out of her life after that.

Her mom stroked her head. "I know your cousin isn't the easiest to get along with, but my brother said having Louise marry first between all the cousins has set her on edge a bit. And now that you and Trent are so serious, I'm sure she's feeling the pressure even more."

"If that's Veronica under pressure, I hate to see what she's like when she's in full-on stressed out mode," she grumbled.

Her mom chuckled. "Well, hopefully we won't have to find out. And speaking of Trent, you should have him come by tonight. I'd love to meet this special guy of yours."

"Meet? Tonight? Oh, no, that can't happen," she blurted without thinking.

"Why not?"

Yeah, Maddie. Why on earth not? "Uh, because…" she said, searching frantically for a plausible explanation. "He works. And he has to go out a lot when he works. At night." Lame, but not necessarily a lie. In fact, Trent might even be out on another date at that very moment, which for some reason kind of irked her. Was it unreasonable to ask he remain a monogamous escort while he was under contract with her?

"Don't you plan on seeing your boyfriend at all before the wedding?"

Not if I can help it. Little did her mother know that she hoped to delay being in Trent Montgomery's macho-football presence for as long as possible. But she supposed if she and Trent were seriously seeing each other, they would make time for each other. "Uh, yeah. Sure."

"Good. Then before you go out, Trent can certainly spare some time to sit and visit with your old mom here. We can all have a nice chat. How does that sound?"

"That sounds…" *Nightmare-on-Elm-Streetish.* "Perfect."

She gulped. She and Trent hadn't gone over anything personal about each other yet. They still needed to get their stories straight.

She'd have to scramble to see if Trent was even available to stop by. It would probably just require thirty minutes of his time. She was sure the great Money Montgomery could spare a measly half an hour to ensure this job goes smoothly. Oh, crap, would he charge extra?

Her mom stood. "It'll be good to get to know him before the wedding."

"You're telling me," she muttered, but she must have

said it louder than she'd thought, because her mom gave her a strange look. "I mean, it'll be good for *you* to get to know him." She gave a shaky little laugh. "I'll call him right now."

Maddie picked up her cell phone in front of her mom, making it look as if she were going to do just that. She even had her index finger poised in the call-ready position.

Too bad she didn't actually have Trent's number.

Her mom clasped her hands together. "I'll chill some wine just in case he's free. Does he prefer red or white?"

Maddie held in a scream. Her mom was killing her with all these questions about Trent. Slowly and painfully killing her.

"I don't think it matters, Mom." She hoped. And she hoped he was available.

"Okay, I'll give you and your man some privacy then." Her mother practically floated to the door then, with a bright smile, closed it behind her.

As soon as she heard the click of the doorknob, Maddie scrolled through her contact list in her phone until she found Kennedy's number. Hopefully, this extra little "service" she was about to ask for wouldn't be an issue. She was in too deep now to turn back. She needed to make this wedding date look like a real relationship. Hopefully, Trent wasn't already booked.

Without wasting another second, she hit the dial button and waited for Kennedy to pick up, all the while wondering if this was what it felt like to lose one's mind.

"You're late," was all she said in greeting.

Trent glanced at his cell phone. He was one minute ahead of the time Kennedy had told him to report to Maddie's house. He inhaled deeply.

Serenity now.

The things he put up with for family. Maddie and Kennedy were damn lucky the only thing he had going on tonight was giving his dog a bath, otherwise he would not be on this woman's doorstep about to play devoted boyfriend.

Although, seeing the way Maddie looked when she answered the door more than made up for her sour attitude. From her blond hair pulled back in a low ponytail to the sleeveless pink T-shirt dress with white flip-flops, Maddie looked as good and smelled as sweet as one of those petit fours his mom would always serve at her fundraiser teas. Maddie was the epitome of the girl next door. The one he'd always ignored all throughout school. Not his usual type. However, he couldn't deny the fact that Maddie McCarthy was a natural traffic stopper.

He slipped his phone back into his pocket and held out his arms. "Is that any way to greet your adoring boyfriend?"

She shot him a glare that could have easily taken down the best of linebackers. "Just get in here. We need to discuss some things before my mo—"

"There he is," an older woman said in a sing-song voice. "The man of the hour."

Maddie's cheeks colored. "Oh, Mom." She nervously glanced from her mother to him. "Yes, this is Trent. Um, ta-da!"

Maddie's mom looked young, maybe early fifties. She was attractive with straight blond hair that just brushed her shoulders, and she had a trim figure like her daughter. She walked up to him and took his hand firmly between her own. "It's so nice to meet you."

Trent smiled back. "You, too." And he found he meant it. Maddie's mom seemed like a sweet woman who loved and was concerned for her daughter. Very unlike his own mother, who ignored him most of his life until he became a college football star and she could brag to anyone within a three foot radius. His mom was more the rich, pampered type whose version of natural childbirth meant giving birth without makeup. His father wasn't far behind in that belief. His parents weren't even there for him when Trent had suffered his accident in college. Only Kennedy had given him the moral support he'd needed during his recovery and then his decision to quit football. He would never forget that, which was why he would do anything for his cousin now, including posing as a boyfriend/wedding date to a high-strung blonde who seemed to hate him.

"My sneaky little daughter has been hiding you from us for quite a while," her mom went on.

Trent lifted an eyebrow at Maddie, who went pale at her mom's "hiding" comment. "Yes, our Maddie here is a crafty one all right," he agreed. "In fact, you'd be surprised at some of the things I've seen her try to pull off recently."

Maddie wound her arm through his, slyly digging her thumbnail into his biceps. "Now, *honey*, you don't need to go spilling secrets," she said between clenched teeth.

"Oh, come now," he said, patting her hand, "there shouldn't be secrets between family, right?" Her eyes went wide, and he bit down on a laugh. Yes, he had probably tortured this poor woman enough all through school, but heaven help him, he couldn't resist having a little fun with her. It had been way too long since he'd wanted to laugh out loud like this. He liked her feistiness.

Blue-eyed fury stared back at him. "Well, if you do spill secrets, I might have to tell a few of my own. Like your Viagra story."

Her mom half cleared her throat, half choked. "You know, now might be a good time for a glass of wine." Fanning her face, she turned and made her way down the hall.

Maddie rushed to follow, but he grabbed her hand, yanking her back. "Not so fast. *Viagra* story?"

"What?" She had the nerve to bat her eyelashes. "You were the one getting cute, hinting around to me hiring you for Louise's wedding. Besides," she said with a smug grin, "it was the first thing that popped in my head when I looked at you."

"Thanks a lot. You gave your mom the idea that I have 'performance' problems."

She shrugged. "It's fine. She'll only assume I'm with you for more than just your body."

"Well, from now on, I'd prefer you to be more shallow."

"Like all those cheerleaders you dated in high school?"

"Ah," he said, wagging a mocking finger at her, "I figured since we've gone from the dating to relationship phase in less than twenty-four hours, you'd see how committed I am. Obviously you're the jealous type."

"Look, just don't try anything else funny. It's not too late for me to fire you."

Trent was all too tempted to call her on that. By his account, it *was* too late. Unless she wanted to show up to her sister's wedding stag, which he highly doubted considering this whole big ruse she was trying to pull off in the first place. But he wisely decided to keep his mouth shut and keep the peace for the sake of his cousin. "Anything you say, boss."

She regarded him through wary eyes. "All right then. This shouldn't take too long. I told my mom we would have one drink with her. Just follow my lead and pretend we've been dating for months then when I tap my watch, you'll mention that we have to get going because we have dinner reservations. Can you handle that?"

I can handle anything you want to give me, Trent's mind suggested. Then he gave his hormones a swift mental slug. What the hell? He was supposed to be thinking of Maddie as a job. A favor to his cousin and business arrangement only. That was *all.*

But his gaze still traveled up her pink dress, past her tanned arms and graceful smooth neck, to capture her pretty-as-a-picture—albeit annoyed looking—face, framed by long blond waves.

"Trent, did you hear me?"

"Huh? Oh yeah, I can handle that."

"No, I said in case my mom asks what restaurant we're going to, say The Crab House."

He quickly pulled himself out of his Maddie daydream and put on his business face. He should at least try and *look* professional. "Right. The Crab House. Got it."

She gave him a long look before nodding. "Are you okay?"

"Of course." And he would be. He may have found Maddie McCarthy an attractive woman, but that didn't mean he wanted any serious involvement with her. She definitely seemed like a marriage-minded woman, and marriage was one thing he was not interested in. At least not anymore.

Candace had taught him all those promises of love and forever didn't mean much. Just pretty talk. Plus, now was not the time to add complications to his life when he should be concentrating on his gyms and, although he barely knew Maddie, he had a feeling "complicated" was her middle name.

He offered her his arm. "Let's get this mother inquisition started."

She hesitated a moment then slipped her arm through his. "Just remember, I lead, you follow."

"Okay, but when we're dancing at the wedding, I lead, you follow."

She sighed dramatically. "I guess I can agree to that."

He chuckled. "See? I have a feeling this is the beginning of a beautiful fake relationship."

She worried her bottom lip as they walked toward the kitchen together. "I'm sure glad one of us feels that way."

Chapter Four

Maddie sat on the couch sandwiched between her mom and Trent and wished for a 5.0 earthquake. Considering any kind of earthquake was a rarity in New England, she had to settle for the mere hope that her mom wouldn't ask any more personal questions and that she and Trent could smoothly make their exit within the next ten minutes.

Her mom took a small sip of Chardonnay and smiled. "So how did you two meet up again?"

"A friend," she said at the same time Trent said, "High school."

Maddie glared at Trent. Didn't she mention many times over that *he* was to follow *her* lead?

She grabbed his hand and gave it a warning squeeze. "I think what we both mean to say, Mom, is that we got together through a friend who we both knew in high school. She set us up and voilà, we sort of clicked."

Key phrase being *sort of*.

Trent threw an arm around her and pulled her to his side. He seemed comfortable playing the part of her boyfriend. A little too comfortable. Probably had lots of escort practice. Maddie reluctantly settled into him and couldn't help catching a noseful of what could only be described as "essence of male deliciousness"—consisting of whatever soap Trent used mixed with the man himself. She averted her face and tried not to let his scent cloud her brain from the task at hand.

"We must have clicked. I can honestly say I never jumped into a relationship so fast before in my entire life," he said with a chuckle.

Maddie gritted her teeth. One more cute comment like that and Mr. Stand-up Comic was going down. Trent obviously suffered too many blows to the head during football in college. He wasn't following her direction at all. What was she paying him for? It didn't matter how good he looked or how freaking fantastic he smelled. He was the worst hired boyfriend/wedding date ever!

Her mom nodded. "You can't fight chemistry. And you two definitely have it."

We do? Maddie looked at Trent, who shot her a slow wink and ran a caressing hand down her arm. Yowsa. Okay, so maybe the man did know how to do his job well. He certainly had enough "practice" in high school.

"So, Trent, what do you do for a living?" her mom asked.

Oh, no. Her most feared question. She wrung her hands. *Please don't say male escort, please don't say male escort.*

Trent smiled. "I'm the owner of Red Zone Fitness gym downtown. In fact, I opened up two others along the North Shore within the last year or so."

"How wonderful," her mom said.

Maddie's pulse began to quiet. A business owner of three gyms was a pretty good cover. She nudged him with her elbow. "Nice," she whispered.

Trent looked confused for a second then continued to address her mom. "It seemed like a natural fit for me with my business degree and my love of sports and fitness after I couldn't play football anymore."

Her mom nodded. "Yes, we were sorry to hear about the accident. It's a shame it affected your health and your career."

"Yeah, playing pro ball was a dream that wasn't meant to be. It was a tough decision, but I suffered too many concussion symptoms after that last hit. It wasn't worth the risk to my life. At least it wasn't worth the risk to me," he added quietly, but Maddie caught the bitterness in his tone.

Maddie lowered her gaze. She didn't want to feel sympathy toward Trent Montgomery, but she could imagine it was tough for him to give up on his dreams like that. As much as she wanted to hate him for being such a stuck-up spoiled rich boy in high school, she couldn't. Not when he looked so dejected, talking about what he could have had. She wondered if that was the reason he got mixed up in the escort business in the first place: in order to fill some attention void.

Her mom sighed. "It's so nice that you two got together again after all these years. Maddie had the worst things to say about you in high school. But I suppose she didn't really know you, and you both were so young."

Trent narrowed his eyes, a hint of a smile hovering over his lips. "Oh, yeah? What kinds of things did she say about me?"

"D-darling," Maddie sputtered, "does it even matter anymore? I mean it's all in the past, right?" That's all she needed was her mom going on and on about every name in the book she'd called Trent when they were in high school. Their fake relationship was on edge enough.

Trent smiled down at her. "Of course it's in the past," he said, patting the back of her hand. Then his gaze shot to her mom again, direct and businesslike. "So what'd she say about me?"

Her mom bit her lip. "Oh dear. Maybe I shouldn't have opened my mouth."

Yeah, Mom. Way to go. Apparently her curse wasn't limited to *real* relationships. The fake ones were doomed, too.

Then Maddie remembered her lifeline. She tapped her watch and gave Trent a pointed look. It was time to make their exit.

Trent ignored her.

"Did she really hate me?" he asked her mom again.

Maddie held in a scream. Why was he even concerned with how she felt about him in high school? He had more than a few dozen allegiant girl fans back then to feed his ego. She cleared her throat—loudly—and began tapping her watch again.

That's the signal, dumb-dumb. Let's go.

Her mom frowned. "Is your watch giving you trouble, dear?"

"No," she said with a sigh. "My watch is fine."

It was the fake boyfriend who was the trouble.

The man couldn't take a cue if he was hit over the head with it—which she wasn't far off from doing. "I, uh, happened to notice the time. Trent and I have dinner reservations tonight." She turned to Trent. "We should get going, shouldn't we, *honey*?"

"Yes, of course." He stood smoothly and held out his hand to help her up. "So nice to meet you, Mrs. McCarthy. I look forward to talking with you more at Louise's wedding."

Maddie rolled her eyes. Yeah, right. There was no way he was going to talk anymore with her mom—or to anyone. At least, not if she could help it. She hoped he would be eye candy and nothing else.

Her mom beamed. "It was so nice to finally meet you. Have a nice dinner, you two."

"Thanks, Mom. Don't wait up," she grunted, shoving Trent toward the door, which was no easy feat, since he had to have a good seventy pounds of muscle on her.

She stumbled out the door, pulling Trent with her, then gave one last wave good-bye to her mom and shut the door behind them. "Okay, what was that all about?" she whispered heatedly.

Trent raised his eyebrows at her. "What was *what* all about?"

"You," she said, poking him in the chest with each word, "were supposed to follow my lead."

He folded his arms and chuckled. "Ah, so you wanted a puppet."

"*Puppet?*" The nerve. Like she was one of those self-serving control-freak women. As if. "That's not what I meant at all, hotshot. All I wanted was for you to not speak unless spoken to, and if you do speak then you follow my cues."

"Right." He cocked an eyebrow then looked down at her with that all-too-knowing grin. When she felt a responding smile start in her chest, she itched to smack his grin off his all-too-handsome face.

"We need to be on the same page here, Trent. You can't keep going rogue on me, or we'll never survive next week."

He shrugged his broad shoulders. "Can't help it. Quarterback instinct. When I see an opportunity for a new play that will work better, I'm going to take it. It's called calling an audible."

Of course Trent had to make everything about football. She resisted the urge to hum "Glory Days" and checked her watch instead. That little episode with her mom lasted all but thirty minutes, yet she felt as if she'd sprinted a half marathon. They really were going to have to do some homework on each other if this was going to go off without any more hitches. She couldn't afford for it not to. "Look, I think that if we—"

But before she'd gotten the rest of her words out, Trent Montgomery's lips landed on hers with the precision of a military sniper.

There he went again, going rogue on her.

Although…truth be told, this time she didn't mind so much.

Trent slid his hands up her back and pulled her even closer in to him. *Oh, mama,* but the man could kiss even better than he could throw a football, and if she had a pair of pompons handy, she could definitely drum up a few cheers at the moment. His mouth moved against hers in a perfect combination of softness and confidence. Gosh, it had been so long since a man had kissed her like this. Really kissed her. She wove her arms around his neck and had to remind herself it was all wrong. Trent Montgomery had tons of women at his disposal, she had hired him for a job, to escort her to her sister's wedding only. But the hard press of him against her, his hands in her hair, it all felt so right.

A moment went by before she realized he'd pulled back to look at her. "Sorry about that," he murmured.

"Mm-hmm." Wait. What? *He's sorry?*

"I saw your mom through the window, and I didn't want her to see us arguing."

"Oh," she uttered lamely. "G-good thinking."

Right. That was why Trent had kissed her. Of course. Because he was trying to play the part of her boyfriend in front of her mother. Not because he really *wanted* to kiss her. Which was fine—perfect even—because she didn't want him kissing her, either. Why would she? There wouldn't be any future in it. But she turned away in case the burning sensation in her cheeks could be seen in the setting sun.

He reached out and took hold of her hand. "Hey, are you okay?"

"Never better," she lied. Or she would be better when she finally got away from Trent's presence. She needed to regroup. The man not only did things to her mind but her insides as well.

"I don't normally kiss women without asking them first."

"Good to know." She shook off his hand. She could keep this just as businesslike as he could. "Thank you for meeting my mom on such short notice. I'll be in touch after the weekend." And with that, she congratulated her legs for making it down the porch steps and halfway down the brick walkway. He called her name before she made it to her car.

"What?"

He cocked his head and sent her a dimpled smile. "Where are you going in such a hurry?"

Where am I going? "I don't know. Probably the library."

"On a Friday night?" He made a show of horror. "What the heck are you going to do there?"

"Oh, what most people do at their local library—three way orgy, summon up the dead, if there's time, jam up the copy machine with Canadian quarters. Same old same old."

He laughed. Damn her traitorous insides, because the deep rumbling wound her up tighter than she was already feeling after that kiss. So not good.

"How about we grab something to eat instead?" he suggested.

Eat? As in spend-more-time-together eat? Oh, capital-H-hell no.

Trent seemed to read her mind, because he was already walking over to her, stating all the reasons in favor of such an idea. "Plus, if you want this thing to look as real as possible, we need to get to know each other better. I don't even know how you take your coffee."

"That's because I don't drink coffee."

"See? This is stuff a real boyfriend should know. I take mine black with one sugar, in case you were wondering."

"I wasn't." She folded her arms, not wanting to be amused.

His gaze was steady as he leaned in to her, his voice dipping an octave lower. "Well, maybe there are other things you're wondering about me."

She tried to swallow and realized she couldn't because her mouth had gone bone dry. As much as her mind was telling her Trent had a good point about them getting to know each other, her insides were telling her he was dangerous to her, too. But since she was never the smartest in her class, her brain finally won out.

"Oh, all right," she murmured. "I suppose we could grab something *quick* to eat. I guess…"

"You might want to dial down the enthusiasm. My big head won't be able to fit in the car."

Though she tried not to, she gave in to a chuckle. She supposed being amused by his sarcastic commentary didn't have to mean that she forgave his behavior in high school or that they were now friends. But he was being unusually kind in trying to help and work with her, so the least she could do was not be rude. "Sorry. Dinner sounds like a good idea."

"Great. We'll go to Duke's on Second Street. My treat. Hopefully they'll still have some booths available where we'll be able to talk in private and get to know each other's idiosyncrasies. I'll be the best fake wedding date you've ever had."

Maddie could only nod as she followed him to his silver Land Rover. She had more pressing issues on her mind than being reminded of her sister's upcoming wedding. Like why she couldn't shake that pretend kiss of his and what was it that she'd really just agreed to.

Trent blamed the impromptu kiss he shared with Maddie for his poor decision-making by offering to take her out.

It was as if his vocal cords had ushered out a dinner in-vite to her before his brain had any say in the matter. He was supposed to be thinking about Maddie in business terms only. But after taking in those plump lips of hers so freshly kissed, all he could think about was kissing her again. He'd admitted to himself earlier that there was something about her he'd liked beyond the superficial qualities that attracted most men. He couldn't explain it, but Maddie had an effect on him that he hadn't felt since his engagement. Maybe never.

And he didn't care for it one bit.

She happened to look up from her burger and caught him staring. "Oh, no. I have ketchup on my face, don't I?" She grabbed a bunch of napkins and began furiously wiping her mouth.

"There's no ketchup."

Her eyes widened. "Oh crap. Mustard? That's worse."

He smiled. "There's nothing on your face." *Except pretty rosy cheeks and bright blue eyes.* He cleared his throat and took a gulp of his beer. "Let's pick up where we left off."

Maddie nodded and pushed her plate away. "Now you know a little bit about my sister and mom. And we know how we met up and what you do for a living. Owning a bunch of gyms was a brilliant lie, by the way."

"Thanks, but that wasn't a lie. I do happen to own three Red Zone Fitness gyms in the North Shore area."

Maddie stilled. "*You do?* But I thought…"

"You thought what?"

Her cheeks grew even rosier as she fidgeted in her seat. "Uh, nothing."

"What?"

"Nothing."

"Maddie," he said in a warning tone, "did you think I worked solely for Match Made Easy?"

"Ye—no." She gave a fake laugh then swallowed hard. "*No.* Of course not."

Trent looked up at the ceiling and sighed. He wasn't

sure if he should feel insulted or flattered that she thought he could actually make a decent full-time living as a paid male escort. She still must not think very much of him. He wanted to tell her he'd changed, that he wasn't the same self-centered kid he was in high school. Although it killed him not to defend himself and tell her he was only pretending to be a male escort for his cousin's matchmaking company, he and his cousin had a lot riding on this gig. It shouldn't matter what Maddie thought about him, anyway.

But in a small way, it kind of did.

Maddie bit her lip. "If you don't mind my asking, how did you end up doing"—she gestured wildly between the two of them—"this?"

He briefly thought back on his cousin coming to him when she was in college, bright with enthusiasm, telling him about her new idea for a business and begging him to invest. "You could say it kind of found me," he hedged. And that was about all he could say. If Maddie kept poking around and ever found out he wasn't an escort and didn't even hold an escort license, it could spell trouble for his cousin's business if she decided to take her to court or if word ever got out.

"Ah, like how Sharon Parker's bra kind of found its way into your locker?"

He leaned in, resting his elbows on the table. "Are you going to constantly bring these things up the entire time we're dating?"

"Sorry. Just using my prior knowledge to try and gauge what kind of fake boyfriend you're going to make."

"Well, if your bitterness is any indication of the kind of fake girlfriend you're going to be, I won't hold my breath for you to fake put out."

She slid him an amused look. "Good. As long as we're both going into this thing with low expectations, there'll be no disappointments."

"Let's leave high school in the past, shall we, and get back to creating information about our fake relationship?"

She frowned but eventually nodded. "Well, you heard about Louise and you met my mom. What about your parents? What should I know?"

He couldn't say, considering he rarely spoke to them since graduating college. He became a bit of a disappointment to them when he was no longer making the sports page. Was it any real wonder he was such a bastard growing up when he had such superficial role models?

"My father is the chief of staff at Mass General and my mother enjoys her charity work and serving on some community boards in town," he said evenly.

"Are you close with them?"

He hesitated. "No."

"But aren't you an only child?"

"What's that got to do with anything?"

"I—I just thought that only children were supposed to be close to their parents. You know, the parents often shower all their love on one child because they can't spread the attention around to the siblings."

"Would have been kind of hard to spread the love when there wasn't much to go around in the first place."

"What do you mean?"

"I mean that most of my life I've been treated as more of a trophy to have in their ordered little world than an actual human being. Until I went to kindergarten, I actually thought the nanny *was* my mom. When I started to find a niche in football, that's when my parents decided to reenter my life. Maybe they wanted to ride on the wave of my success. Who knows? Whatever the reason, it actually worked out well for a time. For all of us. I had a family, and they had something to brag about in their social circles. Unfortunately, like all good things, it came to an end when my doctor told me I would have to consider no longer playing football."

Her brows knitted together as she took in all that he'd told her. "I'm so sorry. I had no idea. You always seemed like you had everything growing up."

"Yeah. I guess it would have looked that way." Trent looked down when he felt warmth on his hand and saw that Maddie had covered it with her own. Her hand seemed so delicate, yet carried a weight of comfort for such a small package. Her fingers entwined with his. She seemed lost in thought, and he wondered if she even realized what she was doing.

Trent suddenly couldn't breathe. He couldn't believe he'd shared that information about his parents with her. He wanted to keep this fake relationship simple. Not get attached. He was determined to never go down that route again. The lesson he'd learned from his ex-fiancée still burned in his memory. Love wasn't constant. It was conditional. Which was why he avoided long-term relationships at all costs.

"Wow, I never thought you—" Maddie's gaze fell on their joined hands. She abruptly pulled away. "It's late," she said.

"Is it?" he asked, trying to mask his disappointment.

She bit her lip. "Yeah. Actually, I have somewhere to be in the morning, and you've put in enough overtime for this job. Plus, we've been out long enough to fool my mom, right?"

He nodded and signaled to the waitress. Maddie was right. It was a good idea to call it a night. They had been out long enough to fool her mom.

And long enough to almost fool himself.

Chapter Five

Maddie breathed a sigh of relief when Trent arrived to pick her up the following Tuesday. She had been waiting by the curb of her house clutching a suitcase in each hand. Not that Trent was late by any means. She was extra jittery. Today marked the first day of festivities planned by her sister's future in-laws and the introduction of Trent as her wedding date. She hoped both she and Trent could survive the week without mishap.

Trent pulled over. He looked about to get out, but she yanked open the passenger door and threw her luggage and garment bags in the back before his hand could reach the handle.

"Good morn—"

"Hurry," she urged. She slammed her door closed and scrunched down in the seat.

"Hurry?" Trent stared down at her. "You do realize the actual wedding isn't for four more days, right?"

"I know. It's just that I don't want them seeing you."

He scanned the yard. "Who's *them*?"

"My mom and aunt." She crouched farther and gave a few impatient waves toward the steering wheel. "Sheesh, can you please talk and drive at the same time?"

He licked his lips, trying not to be amused at the blond ball of anxiety sitting next to him. "You're the boss," he said, and pulled the car out onto the road.

Maddie glanced back at the house and let out a visible sigh of relief. "That was close."

"I'm confused," he said. "I thought you were hiring me as your wedding date so people would actually *see* you had a wedding date."

"Well, yes, of course, but I can't have everyone bombarding you with more questions. According to what I told everybody, we've already been dating for months, and we can't have a repeat of the other night with my mom. Even though we know a little more about each other than we did, we still need two months' worth of information memorized. And by the way, you're going too fast," she added, bracing a hand on the dashboard.

Trent rolled his eyes but had the decency to take his foot off the gas pedal. "I think I know you well enough already."

"Oh, yeah? What do you think you know?"

"I know that you're a perfectionist and a backseat driver. How am I doing so far?"

She glared at him. "Terribly."

He chuckled. "Okay, why don't you start by telling me about the best man. Your ex."

"Ryan? Why do you want to know more about him?"

He shrugged a shoulder. "I need to be aware of the

competition. Like watching football films of the opposing team before a game. After all, I assume he's the reason you hired a wedding date in the first place. You want to show him you've moved on, right?"

Maddie bit her lip. "Sure, that…and a few other reasons," she murmured.

Like salvaging my pride and refuting the family curse.

The last thing she needed was people whispering behind her back and feeling sorry for her on Louise's special day. The pitying looks were the worst. So she'd convince everyone she was in a serious relationship now and worry about the future later. She could even use Match Made Easy after the wedding and hire Trent out for a few birthdays and around the holidays. Keep the ruse going until she met someone for real. Yeah, that could totally work.

Maybe.

Her nerves were making her sweat, so she opened up the glove compartment hoping he had some tissues stashed there. She pulled out a small bag of dog treats instead. "Are these in case we get the munchies on the drive down?"

"Those are for Bella," he said, grinning.

"Your girlfriend must have really fresh breath then."

"Bella is my *dog*. I don't have a girlfriend."

So he was an animal lover. Huh. She digested that, along with the no-girlfriend bit as she shoved the bag back into the compartment. She didn't know why, but Trent not having a girlfriend didn't compute, especially with the reputation he had in high school. Although for another unknown reason, she wasn't entirely unhappy about that information, either. Plus, she thought it was kind of cute that he kept special treats in his car for his pet. But just *kind of* cute. In a purely non-sexual observational way.

"So what's he like?" he asked again.

"Who?"

He sighed. "Ryan. The infamous ex."

"Oh." She rested her head back and thought for a few seconds as Ryan's handsome face popped into her mind. "For starters, Ryan is extremely attractive. He's committed to his job, loves smooth jazz, skiing, expensive red wine, and is always very punctual."

Trent made a face. "Do men like that really exist? How did you let a dreamboat like that get away?"

Like how they all got away, she wanted to say. The dreaded curse. "He's the head chef at The Ripe Tomato in Charlestown and cheated on me with one of the hostesses."

"Ouch."

She sighed. "It gets worse. I used to work at The Ripe Tomato, too, as head pastry chef. After I found out about his affair, he bad-mouthed me to the owner. Whatever he said must have worked, because I was conveniently laid off not long after that."

"The rat bastard."

"Exactly. And believe me, pastry chef jobs are few and far between. I've had zero luck with interviewing. I'm still searching, but soon I'll have to look out of state."

"Then he's a double rat bastard."

She had to crack a smile at how outraged he sounded for her. The incident happened months ago and, although she had been crazy about Ryan, she had gotten over her heartbreak a lot faster than she had gotten over him getting her fired. But maybe she was more used to her relationships blowing up on her.

"It was a hard lesson learned," she murmured.

"What lesson was that?"

"Never get involved with anyone you work with. You might want to take my advice." She pointed a finger at him and added, "Especially in *your* line of work."

That frat boy grin returned. "I'll keep that in mind."

She sat back and sighed. "Needless to say, it's going to be extra nice to show up with you on my arm and rub his nose in it. But in order to do that, we need to look happy and in love. I mean, *you* really need to look in love. Like I'm your whole world."

"That's why you're paying me the big bucks."

"You can say that again," she muttered. Her dwindling bank account proved it. But it would be worth it to see the shock on Ryan's face and not see those pitying looks from her family.

He glanced at her with a frown. "You know, out of curiosity…since I didn't have time to look at the contract… how much are you paying for me anyway?"

"Three thousand dollars."

"*Three thousand dollars?* Are you crazy?"

She narrowed her eyes. "What are you talking about? Kennedy told me that was a fair price."

"Uh, I mean…" He coughed and cleared his throat. "Yeah, she must have given you a special. I usually go for way more than that."

She watched him a moment. Not that she really wanted to know how much other women were willing to pay for Trent Montgomery's services, but she couldn't help uttering, "I suppose you must get hired for weddings like this all the time."

He braked for a red light, his hands tightening around the steering wheel. "No, actually. I don't. Kennedy knows I don't do weddings."

"Don't do them or don't like them?"

"Both."

She blinked. "Really? So you never go to weddings?"

"Nope." His gaze traveled over to her, and something in those hazel eyes of his shifted. "I made an exception in your case."

She swallowed as he continued to stare at her. The air around them began to swirl with heat, fogging her mind about him even more. It was silly for her to feel special that he was doing something he didn't ordinarily do for her sake. After all, she was paying him good money and this was just a simple job to him. Nothing else.

She turned her head and cracked the window. "Lucky me," she said dryly. "And I wasn't even waving any pompons when you agreed to this job, either."

"You know, I don't remember you being this bitter in high school."

She snorted. "That's because you don't remember me at all."

The light turned green, and he pressed the gas pedal. The car ride went silent after that. Maddie decided it was probably for the best. They were going to be stuck together for a good chunk of the week, so a break from talking would be good. Besides, the more she talked with Trent the more he confused her. Any man who stored treats in his car for his dog couldn't be all that heartless. She recalled the way he had opened up to her at dinner a few days ago and was shocked to learn his family life was just as turbulent as hers only for different reasons. Apparently, the rich boy with the golden arm and self-centeredness the size of Indiana was just as miserable as she was growing up.

Looks were definitely deceiving. But at this point, that was what she was counting on to get her through her sister's wedding. She just had to remember to keep everything in perspective. A girl—even a relationship-cursed girl—had to have her standards. She would never really date someone like Trent, a man still so full of himself that he decided to "rent" himself out to women for money on the side. Not really surprising he would choose to do that when she thought back on how he used to be. Well, Trent may still have that panty-removing charm from high school, but she wasn't about to fall under *that* spell again.

After thirty minutes of listening to the radio without talking, Trent finally reached out and turned it off. "Okay, so tell me more about yourself."

"Like what?"

"Like what it is that I should be so smitten over? So far I've only experienced your backseat driving skills and silent treatment talents."

She lifted her chin. "Hey, I can be very charming."

"That has yet to be determined," he countered. Although he held a grin when he said it.

"Well, animals and children happen to love me."

He yawned.

"I'm a fantastic cook, too."

Trent made a right down a long, landscaped drive along the bay, where the groom's parents had their estate. A little sliver of nervousness began to creep up her spine. They didn't have much more time to get their story straight or know each other and prove to everyone that they had been in a relationship for months.

"I can make a mean chocolate ganache," she blurted. "It's delicious and so spreadable."

His interest seemed peaked. "Spreadable chocolate?" he said with a sizzling smile. "Now we're talking. And what exactly do you do with this spreadable ganache of yours?"

"Frost cupcakes."

His shoulders wilted. "I'm losing fake interest fast, Maddie. I can act but you better give me something better to work with here, or we're both in trouble. Use your imagination a bit."

For Pete's sake, he was right. She couldn't invent an interesting relationship if her life depended on it. Was it any wonder why men didn't stick around? She was even getting bored with herself. "I, um, never had braces and I have perfectly straight teeth."

Straight teeth? That was the best she could come up with? She hung her head in defeat.

He let out a long-winded sigh. "Okay, okay, relax. I think I can work with what you've given me."

She lifted her head. "What do you mean?"

Trent put the car in park and shut off the engine. He sat, staring straight ahead for almost a full minute. Then he finally looked at her. He took hold of her hand, never letting his gaze leave hers. His eyes seared into hers with interest and heat. While she waited for him to speak she had to remind herself to breathe.

His voice dipped low as he leaned in. "Perhaps, Maddie, I'm so infatuated with you because of your heart for animals and kindness toward children. I love that you're the kind of woman who enjoys cooking so we can have intimate dinners together at home. You're a strong woman but not to the point of wearing the pants in a relationship. You're funny and love to laugh but not at the expense of others. Injustice drives you crazy, and you'll fight to the death if anyone threatens your sister or someone you love. Yes, your teeth are straight except for your left incisor, which leans slightly to the right. Your eyes are clear blue but when you get mad or excited they take on a sea-greenish tint. And when I take you in my arms, I wonder how on earth I ever survived without knowing what that felt like before I met you."

She blinked back tears at his beautiful words and was astonished that he could presume to know her as well as he did. Somehow he managed to capture so many things about her that were true. Her lungs felt squeezed of all air, but she managed to whisper, "Yeah, let's go with that."

He sent her a simmering smile and kissed her knuckles. "I like to think I know women."

His words crashed into their lovely moment like a cell phone going off in the middle of a funeral service. But then she realized that what he created was just that: made up and completely unreal. He apparently did know women well and what they wanted to hear. She should have known Trent Montgomery was still the same smooth-talking game-playing kind of guy he was in high school. In fact, she should thank him for the reminder. She was a fool to think for that brief second that he really liked her or knew anything about her. They weren't in high school anymore. Unfortunately, there were still some remnants of that old schoolgirl crush she had for him that were unresolved.

She had to trample those feelings. Fast. Trent

Montgomery had no interest in her then and obviously had even less interest now. The only reason he said those romantic things about her was because she was paying him to do so. Period.

She yanked her hand back and stomped out of the car. As soon as she did, she saw Louise fly out of the mansion, all smiles and excitement to meet her sister's wedding date. Her sister's *hired* wedding date.

Maddie lifted a hand and gave her a limp wave. She prayed Louise would not see through their ruse. Biting her lip, she sent a nervous glance over to Trent, who had already gotten out of the car. His stance and expression remained calm. The same look he had whenever he'd set foot on a football field. He nodded at her, rubbing his hands together as if he had a play in mind and was about to call out cadence.

At least someone had confidence in what we're doing, she thought, crossing her fingers. *Now let the real game begin.*

Trent glanced at Maddie's annoyed stance and wondered if his football dreams weren't the only thing he'd lost years ago. His finesse with women along with his sanity, apparently, had gone down the toilet as well.

Maddie was giving him the cold shoulder now. Not that he blamed her. As fast as he'd complimented her, he had swiped it all back. But he had to.

Something had shifted inside him when he gazed into her crystal blue eyes. Those eyes of hers that had drunk in everything he said about her like she'd never heard such words before. He hadn't know Maddie for that long, but he could tell she was the kind of woman who wore her heart and emotions on her sleeve. The way she looked at him, like he had scored the game-winning touchdown. That's when he realized he'd said too much. Too much for only a hired wedding date to say. Judging by the way she was in high school and the fact that she needed to hire a wedding date, she probably hadn't heard compliments like that from a man too often. He didn't want a woman like her getting attached to him. A woman who was definitely looking for a wedding of her own. Well, he was the wrong man for *that* particular job. So he corrected his mistake and played it off as no big deal. He brought the moment back to where their relationship should stay: purely professional. After all, Maddie was paying him money to be her pretend date, not a real one.

Before he could gather another thought about Maddie and how he could correct the situation, a younger, shorter version of Maddie—whom he could only assume was her sister—rocketed toward him, launching herself into his arms. Trent played quarterback in college, but luckily for her sake, he'd started out as a wide receiver in high school.

"Oh, I'm so happy to meet you!" she said, giggling as he stumbled back a few steps.

"Uh, the feeling is mutual," he grunted. At maybe five feet two inches tall, Louise could be described as a *fun-sized* version of her sister, but he'd bet she also had a good ten pounds extra on Maddie, too.

"Louise, please," Maddie admonished. "We're only dating. There's no need to start welcoming him into the family quite yet."

Face flushed, Louise took a step back, brushing the blond strands of hair from her cheeks. "Oh, of course. I'm sorry. I didn't mean to scare you off. But we all only learned about you last week so, needless to say, I was super excited to hear that Maddie was in a relationship and that she was bringing you to my wedding. I don't even know your name." She laughed.

"I'm a little hurt she wasn't talking me up more." He cast a side glance toward Maddie. "I'm Trent, by the way. Trent Montgomery."

"It's good to—" Louise's brows slammed together. "Oh, wait. Trent Montgomery? There was a Trent Montgomery in our high school. Are you him?"

"I am."

Louise covered her mouth with her hand, laughing. "Oh my gosh. Too funny. I guess you know my sister used to completely hate you."

He cocked his head at Maddie, pretending to be puzzled. "Did she now?"

Maddie's eyes grew wide. "Um, to set the record straight, I don't know if I ever uttered the word hate."

"Oh yeah, you did," Louise insisted. "You even called him an egotistical blowhard who couldn't throw a beanbag if his life depended on it, remember?"

Maddie flushed every shade of pink known to Crayola. She opened her mouth, as if she wanted to defend herself again, but no words came out.

Trent raised his brows at her. "Seems as if both of us have faulty memories when it comes to high school."

Maddie quickly recovered and tried to wave the comment away. "Well, it was so long ago. Who can remember anything from back then? Besides, we're both different people now. At least, *one* of us is," she muttered.

Louise playfully shoved her sister. "No wonder you didn't tell me his name. That is hilarious. You look adorable together." She beamed at Trent. "And of course if Maddie's happy, then I'm happy. I just know this one is going to last."

Trent smiled at the obvious love and affection Louise had for her sister. It was nice to see. Something he could relate to well with Kennedy. A lot of people didn't have that kind of support. Trent sure as hell never got it from his parents. Or his own fiancée, for that matter.

"I hope to continue to make your sister happy," he said with a wink. Then he glanced over at Maddie. The smile on her face seemed frozen there and about ready to crack off from the tension emanating from her body. So he decided to help her out a bit and reached for her.

Maddie's body was about as pliant as a two by four but he managed to wrap his arms around her in a manner that looked as if she was a willing participant. "I'm sure Maddie would like to freshen up and change before the cocktail party. Where should I take the bags?"

Louise smacked her forehead with her palm. "Oh, of course! Silly me. I'll show you. This place is crazy big. I've been here at least a half dozen times and I still get lost. Michael's parents put you guys together over in the small carriage house on the right of the property. Very quiet and cozy."

"What?" Maddie stopped walking. "I'm sorry, what was that? *Together?* Trent and I are sharing a room? Is that proper wedding guest etiquette?"

Louise laughed like it was the best joke she'd ever heard. "Of course it is. At first, Michael's parents weren't into it. They're so traditional. But then I explained that nowadays things like that aren't a big deal and that you were probably half living at Trent's place anyway, so there wouldn't be anything new he hasn't seen already. Am I right or am I right?"

Maddie was rendered speechless, and Trent wisely kept his mouth shut as Louise stopped at the door and then swung it open in a flourish. She encouraged them to enter first.

The room was something else, traditionally decorated with a mahogany canopy bed and marble fireplace. There was a full bath and even what looked to be a private deck overlooking the water.

"What do you think?" Louise asked, grinning as if she already knew the answer.

"This is fantastic," Trent said.

Maddie, on the other hand, remained mute, staring at the queen bed as if it had just been pulled from the sewer.

"You don't have to thank me," Louise said brightly. "Well, okay, go ahead."

He couldn't help himself. "Thanks, Sis."

He then grinned at Maddie and nearly laughed out loud when it looked as if she wanted to go for his jugular with a nail file. Yes, he was the devil, taunting her like this, but he kind of liked seeing the bossy and overly organized Maddie off her game. So sue him. Plus, Maddie just looked too darn cute all outraged and indignant and…panic-stricken.

Louise checked her watch. "Well, my job here is done. I need to go and talk to Michael's mom about the cocktail party tonight. I'm hoping we can have it outside since the weather is so nice. Why don't you guys relax for a bit? You can meet everyone later."

Maddie rubbed her head. "Sounds good," she said,

sounding anything but good.

"Okay. See you both later." Louise fluttered her fingers in a quick wave and closed the door behind her.

Maddie dropped her hand and warily looked at him. "Sorry to overreact. Sharing a room with you is fine. It's just a minor blip in my radar I wasn't expecting. No offense."

He shrugged. From what he'd observed about Maddie, he could tell she liked to be ultra-prepared. A trait he shared with her. "Understandable."

Maddie rolled her shoulders and sighed. "What a day so far, huh? I could sure go for a shower."

"Me too," he said without thinking.

Her gaze cut to his, sharp and deep. "I meant *alone.*"

He raised his hands in mock surrender and thankfully managed to keep a straight face. "Me too." Although, maybe—*just maybe*—way back in the deep dark recesses of his male mind, he might not have totally meant alone. But that was his little secret.

As if reading his mind, she narrowed her eyes. "Look, Trent, don't get any funny ideas here," she said wagging a pink-polished finger at him. "I trust you can be a professional despite the sleeping arrangements."

Although annoyed she would automatically lump him in the sexual pervert category, he pretended to think it over. "I believe so."

"Good." She looked around the room. "Oh, darn. We forgot to bring the bags with us."

Even though Maddie held a cocky attitude, there were light smudges of fatigue under her eyes, and she looked a bit pale. They hadn't even gotten through the first day yet. He wanted to lay a reassuring hand on her shoulder, but figured any touchy-feely-like advances—as platonic as he intended—would not be appreciated or welcomed at the moment. In fact, he was pretty sure she could summon up enough energy to sock him squarely in the mouth. But he wanted to make things easier and show her that despite his needling, he did intend to help her. "Listen, you stay here. I'll go and get them for you."

"You don't have to do that. I can grab my own luggage, Trent."

"Think of it as part of my overinflated service," he said, trying to coax a smile out of her.

A few beats went by, but it worked. She smiled at him.

Maddie had a fantastic one. Like a skylight had opened up so sunlight could illuminate the room. Not that he should be noticing her smile at all. Or how fantastic it was. Or how great he felt knowing he'd been the cause of it.

Trent frowned. He barely remembered noticing *any* woman's smile in the past several years. What was going on with him? Had it been that long since he'd been alone with a woman?

Maddie cocked her head. "Is something wrong?"

Yes. But he wasn't sure what. He felt his forehead but it was disappointingly cool. "Uh, no. I should get away from you—I mean, get the bags for you."

"Thanks. That's nice," she said, sweeping her blond curls off her shoulders.

He swallowed as his eyes were drawn to her long, graceful neck. He made himself look away. Dammit! He needed some space. One more second alone and he'd be fawning over how trim her cuticles were.

He jerked his thumb over his shoulder, feeling as if all

the air in the room had been sucked out. "Be right back," he wheezed.

Trent practically dove out the door. It was one thing to admit to himself that he was attracted to Maddie and a whole other bag of cleats to be sharing a bedroom with her and not act on that attraction. He took a deep breath. When he mentioned wanting a shower, he should have emphasized a cold one. *Brutally* cold. He had no idea what Kennedy expected when she talked him into helping her, but keeping this job strictly professional was getting more and more difficult by the minute.

Chapter Six

"I bet everything is going as smooth as a baby's bottom down there," Kennedy chirped over the phone.

Trent transferred his cell to his other ear, turning to gaze out along the spans of the beautiful bayfront property. Not too shabby a place to have a party. While Maddie was in the shower, he'd dressed in his dinner jacket and tie and left the room. He figured he'd give her some privacy to get ready for the cocktail party. In the meantime, he'd check in with his cousin while he waited for Maddie to meet him. The weather was perfect, and couples were already outside mingling and hanging around a bar that had been set up by the pool. "Oh, yeah, it's been a real behind all right."

Kennedy chuckled. "Well, somebody tied his necktie too tight. It can't be *that* bad. You only just got there. Unless...of course...you don't get along with Maddie."

"It's not that." More like, he was starting to like Maddie. Not only was she a natural kind of pretty with those ocean-blue eyes of hers, but he admired her spunk, too. It was refreshing to be around a woman who held no pretense or guile and pulled no punches. What you saw with Maddie was pretty much what you got. Unlike his ex-fiancée who pretended to have feelings for him and evidently liked the idea of being married to a football star a heck of a lot more than a gym owner.

"That's good news," she said. "And actually, speaking of good news, I spoke to your dad today."

Trent's spine stiffened. "Why would you call him?"

"He actually called me. He thinks my matchmaking business shows real promise and wants to invest. Can you believe it?"

Trent held his tongue. He didn't want to burst her bubble, but he didn't trust his father's sudden interest in her business—or his interest in anything that didn't benefit or involve himself.

"Trent, you're being awfully quiet. I don't have to see you to know that you're not happy. But don't you get it? If your dad becomes an investor, I'll have the money to pay you back ahead of schedule."

"I plan on talking to the groom about an advertising spot. Everything will work out without my dad's help."

"But I thought you'd be pleased."

"It's not that. It's just…be careful."

She snorted. "I know exactly what I'm doing. Besides, what is there to be careful about? It's family."

Family.

Trent tried not to let the bitterness of that word collect on his tongue. But his parents had no idea what real family entailed, which was why his relationship with them became so strained after he stopped playing football. Kennedy was the only true family he felt he had—the only person he trusted—which was why he'd do anything for her.

He sighed. "Right. It's your business, Ken. I want you to know you don't have to rush to pay me back. I'll figure something out if I can't get the money." And he would. Although he hated to do it, he'd have to close one of his gyms. His line-of-credit business loan was coming due the end of next month. If he couldn't pay it back by then, the bank could start legal action. He hoped it wouldn't come to that. Between his football career and his engagement, he had lost enough already.

She didn't speak for several moments. "You've done so much to help me start my own business. I want to help you now."

His heart squeezed with love for his cousin. "I know. But you've already done enough by just being there for me. Working as a wedding date is the least I can do. How about we call it even?"

"Have I told you you're my favorite cousin?"

He suppressed a grin. He was her *only* cousin. "Not lately."

"Well, you are. Hey, gotta run, I have a client appointment. But I'll call you in a few days. In the meantime, try to pretend that you actually enjoy weddings—if not for Maddie's sake then for mine, please."

"Fine. But I draw the line at the 'Macarena.'"

"Deal."

He clicked his phone off and turned around, almost colliding with a dark-haired woman.

"I'm sorry," he said, reaching out to steady her. "Didn't see you there."

The woman brushed away the hair that had fallen onto her face and looked up with annoyance. But then her eyes widened and her gaze traveled from his face to his chest. "Oh, no problem. It was totally my fault." She licked her overly glossed lips. "Not that I'm really that sorry. You're quite the serendipity to run into."

Trent had been called a lot of things by women over the years, but this one was new to him. "Thanks. Glad no harm done."

She was attractive, but she gave him the immediate impression of a woman who was trying a little too hard by her heavy application of makeup. He smiled and politely tried to step around her, but she shifted and blocked his path. "I'm Veronica."

Oh, crap. This one is a live one. "Trent," he said, taking her outstretched hand.

She didn't readily let go and gave him a look he knew all too well. A look that clearly stated that she'd be ready, willing, and able to meet up with him later if he'd only say the word, which he had no intention of doing. One, he had a job to do—of sorts. And, two, he'd had plenty of *Veronica*s in his day, including his former fiancée. Not a lot of substance to be had. But he had been young and at that time, substance was the last thing he was looking for. He could equate it to having candy for dinner—indulgent, tasty, and fun at first, but then in a few hours, you're longing for a real meal. The woman standing before him was definitely a Snickers bar.

She sidled closer. "I'm the bride's cousin and also one of the bridesmaids. You must be in the bridal party, too?"

"Uh, no, actually, but my date is." He glanced to his left, looking for any outward escape. Then, like a desert oasis,

Maddie popped into view. She looked stunning, wearing a sleeveless aqua dress that made her stand out all the more from the sea of black cocktail dresses surrounding her.

Once she spotted him and Veronica, Maddie wasted no time coming over and planting a chaste kiss on his cheek. "Introducing yourself to my family already I see," she said to him. Then she coolly nodded to Veronica. "Hello, Vonnie. I see you've met my date."

Veronica's mouth dropped. "*This* is the guy you were talking about? Well. No wonder you've been so tight-lipped about him. I'd want to keep him all to myself, too," she said, giving him a long look.

Maddie curled her hands around his arm possessively. "And that's exactly what I plan on doing: keeping him all to myself. You don't mind, do you, honey?" she asked him sweetly.

Trent lifted her hand and kissed the back of it, enjoying the softness of her skin a little more than he should have. "I wouldn't want it any other way."

And he actually meant every word. He was looking forward to spending more time with Maddie. He had convinced himself it was just because he wanted a distraction from all the wedding frenzy, but now he realized, he truly did want to spend time getting to know her better. He wished he could tell her that, along with the fact that he wasn't really a paid escort. But he was afraid it might reflect poorly on Kennedy and her business. It was probably just as well. Better to ignore his attraction to her. It would only be messy when he walked away. Besides, Maddie still seemed like she could barely tolerate his existence.

Veronica ran her tongue over her teeth. "Remind me...

how long have you been together?"

Trent knew this. Maddie drilled it into him enough times on the drive up. He was about to answer but Maddie squeezed his hand. "Oh, it's been about four months or so."

"Wow. A record for you, Maddie," Veronica said. "Maybe the curse is lifting after all."

Curse? Trent frowned. He'd been hearing a lot about this so-called curse and wondered what it all had to do with Maddie.

Maddie seemed to ignore the barb and kept her mild smile in place. "So where is *your* date, cousin?"

"Jeffery got detained in court."

"Another felon? I thought you learned your lesson after last time."

Veronica's lips thinned. "Jeffrey is an *attorney*, not a criminal. And for your information, he'll be here tomorrow night—"

"Great," Trent interrupted. He had decided that was enough of Veronica and her drama. "We should get moving. I promised Maddie's mom we'd go say hello as soon as we got to the party."

Maddie let herself be pulled along for a few moments then dropped his hand and picked up her pace, passing him.

"Hey, hold up," he said.

Maddie turned to him, cheeks flushed and eyes blazing. "What?"

He resisted a smile when a stray curl swung over one eye. The woman was adorable when she was agitated. He stepped closer, placing his hands on her shoulders. "Relax, will you?"

She huffed. "I am relaxed."

"No, you're not. A Zen-like state is not you looking like you're ready to smash more than wedding cake into your cousin's face. You obviously let her get you all worked up and now if anyone sees us together, they're going to think we're fighting. Do you really want that?"

Maddie's shoulders sagged. "Oh, you're right. It's just that she drives me crazy. Her and her little digs. Did you notice her coming on to you? Of course you did. You'd have to be punched in both eyes and deaf not to notice. And right in front of me, too, like I was invisible. It felt like high school all over again, so you'd think I'd be used to it and roll with it better."

Trent cocked his head, trying to put together the Maddie from high school and the Maddie standing before him. It was still hard to believe they were the same person. "You handled yourself all right to me. But just to be safe, better take a few deep breaths."

She closed her eyes and did as he asked. He took the opportunity to study her face, everything from the perfect arch of her brows to her fresh and pretty complexion, and was overcome with a compelling need to brush his lips across each eyelid. Then she opened her eyes, and he almost fell in and drowned in their blue depths.

He cleared his throat. "So, uh, how do you feel?"

"Like shoving my face in a bucket of ice cream."

He chuckled. "That's the spirit."

She closed her eyes and breathed in and out a few more times. "No. Actually, I think I'm good now. Thanks."

"Okay, so tell me, what's this curse I keep hearing about?"

Her eyes widened, glancing everywhere but at him. "Oh,

it's nothing."

"Sounds like nothing is something. And I'd like to hear it from you instead of bits and pieces from your family."

She looked about to deny it again but then flung her hands in the air. "Oh, fine. Just know it's silly. But there seems to be this curse in our family that affects the first-born women. That would be me, in case you haven't guessed from Veronica's not so subtle hint."

Trent grinned. "Wait. Are you telling me that you hired me as your wedding date so people wouldn't think you were cursed?"

"No." She sighed. "Sort of. You see, if people here think I've been in a serious relationship, they won't harp on about the curse thing, and it'll put the focus back where it should be: on Louise and her wedding."

"I see. So you're doing this so they don't focus on the curse. The curse that isn't real."

"Exactly."

"Is this conversation for real?"

Maddie didn't crack a smile. "This isn't funny. If you were approaching thirty-one, had never been in a serious relationship for longer than two weeks, and never been in love before, your family might be on your case about a curse, too. Add in my cheating ex-boyfriend as the best man and you can see that I had to do what I had to do."

"Oh. You mean you freaked out."

She gave him a look. "Yes, I suppose you could call it that. I'm obviously not in a good place in my life right now."

He couldn't help it. The need to soothe and touch her was overwhelming. He lifted his hand to trace the delicate curve of her cheek. "You're with me so you're in the perfect place. And by the way, you're beautiful—inside and out."

She gave him an uncertain smile. "You could have said that in front of my cousin, you know? It would have killed her."

"I'm saying it now."

"But nobody's here to hear it," she said with a nervous catch of laughter.

"You're here," he said huskily.

Her eyes widened as he shifted closer. He knew he shouldn't, but to hell with it. He slipped his arms around her body, could see the pulse racing in her neck. It matched his own racing heart.

She licked her lips but pressed a hand against his chest. "Trent, now is not the time for your games."

"No games," he said, removing her hand from his chest and placing it on his shoulder. "Just a man appreciating the company of his beautiful wedding date." His wedding date he'd been dying to kiss since they'd arrived at the estate. He had wanted her the entire car ride up, fascinated by her testy vulnerability and the way she lit up whenever she talked about her sister and how she wanted the best for her. Maybe even wanted her since he'd seen her trying to fish that diet soda can out of his vending machine.

What would be the real harm in one kiss? he thought. One real kiss with no pretense or anyone watching. One shared kiss between two consenting adults who seemed to have a mutual amount of attraction toward each other. Yes, that was all it would be: one simple kiss. Then he would be completely satisfied and she'd be out of his system.

"I'm going to kiss you," he told her with certainty.

Maddie's eyes flickered with surprise as he leaned in. "I

don't think this is—"

He lowered his mouth to hers, and she responded without hesitation. Her hand gripped the back of his neck. Her touch, her lips, felt so good. Better than he'd imagined. He deepened the kiss, leaning in to her, one hand supporting her back and the other threading his fingers into her hair. With all the unleashed passion he was just getting a sample of, he couldn't for the life of him figure out why this woman didn't have a boyfriend or would ever have to pay for a date. And that, about her, only fascinated him more.

"Oh, excuse me," said a male voice.

Maddie stiffened and was the first to pull back, but Trent refused to drop his arms around her. "Ryan?" she asked.

The man squinted as if he stood fifty yards back instead of merely three feet. "Oh, Madeline. I'm sorry. I was looking for Louise. Veronica told me she was over here."

"Of course she did," Maddie mumbled, shimmying out of his embrace. "H-how are you?"

"Good. It's lovely to see you again." Ryan's gaze shifted to Trent with a look of dismay when Trent slung an arm around Maddie's shoulders.

"Oh, this is my…um, friend, Trent," Maddie offered.

Friend? Trent figured after that kiss they just shared they were definitely out of the friend zone and, for a woman wanting to pretend to everyone here that she was in a relationship, she was doing a lousy job. Did she still have feelings for this nitwit?

Ryan stepped closer and shook Trent's hand. Fancy Boy had to have had a manicure with those kinds of hands, and he wore cuff links. Probably had his shirts custom made. Trent ordered himself to not roll his eyes. Although he could see where some woman might find a refined man like that attractive, Trent also could see that he was not someone who ever played sports or probably exercised, so Trent automatically placed him in the category of "complete tool."

"Your friend?" Ryan eyed Maddie with a level of interest that had Trent's hand closing slowly into a fist. "Well, I hadn't heard that you were bringing anyone to the wedding. That's disappointing."

"Why disappointing?" she asked. "I thought you'd be here with Kristin."

"I broke up with her. I was actually hoping to see you again here... But I guess I had my chance."

"Had it and blew it." His outburst got a look from Maddie, but he didn't care. Fancy-boy Ryan was not going to muscle in on his woman.

His woman? He let his arm slip from her shoulders. Where the hell had that thought come from? Probably from that kiss. Because he hadn't entertained such a possessive thought since his engagement. Why would he? After Candace had left him, he vowed to never put his heart on the line like that again.

Ryan smiled at Maddie. "Well. I guess I should go and try to find your sister."

Maddie nodded. "It's good seeing you."

Ryan turned away and headed toward the pool. After a few moments, Maddie sighed. "Why do I feel the need to be polite? It was not good seeing him. It was torturous. I hope I can avoid him the rest of the night."

"Maybe he'll trip and fall into the pool."

"Ryan can't swim."

"Then I'll push him into the pool."

She let out a laugh, but when she looked up at him, her expression slowly turned serious. "Um, about that kiss... Just curious, but was that for business or for pleasure?"

"Purely pleasure on my end."

"Oh. Um, perhaps we should just keep those things on the business side from now on."

"Things? What things? You mean kisses?"

"Well, yeah. I don't want this arrangement to get mucky, especially since I'm paying you. Don't you agree?"

No. He damn well didn't agree.

But Trent didn't dare voice that thought because only a short week ago he would have completely agreed with her. Part of him even had to wonder if her sudden let's-not-complicate-things talk had anything to do with seeing Ryan again. "Sure. No sense complicating things."

She bit her lip. "Okay then, let's go meet the rest of the family."

He nodded and threaded his hand through hers. She gave him a look but said nothing as they walked along the stone path to the house. *Good*, he thought crossly. Because if she was paying him to be her wedding date, that's what wedding dates did: held hands. And quite frankly, they probably kissed, too. Frequently. And maybe even...

Oh hell.

The shock of discovery hit him with full force. He was completely wrong about Maddie and completely wrong about that one simple kiss. Because she was *not* out of his system and he was *not* satisfied.

Not by a long shot.

Chapter Seven

Maddie had to hand it to Trent. When he wanted to turn on the charm, he really knew how to do it up right. Her aunt Lois and aunt Marie were laughing and hanging on to his every word. Practically eating right out of the palm of his hand. Not that she should be surprised. He certainly charmed enough young girls back in the day. It was only natural that a couple of sixty-year-old women wouldn't be immune.

A cursed thirty-year-old woman wouldn't be immune, for that matter.

Why did Trent have to look so good? Couldn't he have stayed the full-of-himself-jock stereotype? He was nothing like he was in high school. Worse yet, he didn't really fit into the image she had of him being a paid escort. She didn't know what to think anymore. Then again, it was hard to think at all after he'd kissed her the way he had twenty minutes ago.

Despite the whole situation and how he treated her

years ago, she liked him. She really liked him. God-help-her liked him. However, she refused to entertain the idea that Trent was interested in her. The man could have any woman he wanted—and probably did—and she was just... *cursed*. Even on the rarest of rare chances he was interested, so what? It's not like he was looking for a relationship. The man bounced around women in his line of work all the time. Well, she wanted a guy who stuck. She didn't need a fling. She'd had *plenty* of those. A real relationship and a job on the other hand continued to elude her, as her cousin constantly reminded her.

A hand landed on her shoulder, startling her out of her doldrums. "How could someone with such a charming and off-the-scale-hot boyfriend look as if she just heard Ben & Jerry's was going out of business?"

Maddie shot her sister a horrified look. "It isn't, is it?"

Louise chuckled. "Rest assured New York Super Fudge Chunk is safe and sound for the foreseeable future."

"Whew. You had me concerned there for a second."

"Don't evade the question." Her sister's face clouded with concern. "Is everything okay between you and Trent?"

Maddie swallowed hard, becoming increasingly uneasy under her sister's scrutiny. "Nothing could be better. Just look at him," she said, gesturing to where Trent stood, surrounded by adoring gray-haired women. "Everybody loves him."

"Do *you* love him?"

"Love?" She tried but failed to keep the surprise out of her face. "Isn't it a little soon for love?" she choked out. "I mean, we've only been dating a few months."

Louise shook her head. "I've seen the way Trent looks at

you. Besides, Michael and I said the I-love-yous at the three month mark, but honestly, we were ready to tell each other earlier, but we were both too chicken."

Maddie wanted to ask exactly *how* Trent looked at her, but then mentally smacked herself for thinking there was anything beyond their little agreed-upon charade. "Not everyone is as lucky as you and Michael. You guys are going to be the poster children for marital bliss."

Louise squeezed Maddie's hand with a teary smile. "Thank you for saying that."

She frowned and wondered if Louise was holding something back from her. But before she had a chance to ask, Michael's parents were calling her sister over to take some pictures.

"Duty calls," Louise said with her usual cheerful tone.

Maddie watched her sister go then shrugged off the concern when Louise walked right into Michael's arms. Mood lifted, she decided now was the time to rescue Trent from her family. Funny, but even as he carried on a conversation with her aunts, he seemed to be watching her. Waiting for her.

His hand automatically slid around her waist when she approached, and he pulled her into him. She loved the subtle spiciness of his cologne, and a delicious shudder heated her body. She tried to brush off her reaction and not think about how perfectly she molded to his body, but what could she do? She was a weak, weak woman.

"You hit the mother lode with this one, honey," her aunt Marie said, elbowing her a little too hard in her side. Aunt Marie was a tiny woman but, boy, she could produce quite a jab with those bony arms of hers.

"Ladies, you're going to make me blush," he said, grin widening, stretching across his already-too-handsome face.

"Did you know he used to play football?" Aunt Lois added with a dreamy sigh.

Maddie refrained from rolling her eyes. "He might have mentioned it once or twice."

Aunt Lois huffed out a breath. "Once or twice? Goodness, the man is modest, too. Why, he could have been playing for the pros."

"And then we could have been seeing him in his underwear," Aunt Marie added.

Maddie blinked. *"Excuse me?"*

"All good-looking professional athletes do side underwear modeling jobs these days. It's a darn shame women won't be seeing…" Her aunt slid a gleaming gaze down and then up Trent's body. "All that manly physique."

"Is that right?" Maddie raised an eyebrow at him, but he could only offer an unapologetic shrug. She swallowed a giggle, although she couldn't really fault her aunt's disappointment. A body like Trent's should be captured on film. Or by her hands…

Bad Maddie. She should not be thinking about touching Trent's body. Well, maybe just thinking a little bit wouldn't hurt.

Aunt Lois patted Marie's shoulder. "Maddie's seeing it, and that's all that really matters, dear."

"Maybe you could take a picture for us?" Marie asked with hopeful eyes.

"Marie!" Lois barked.

"What? It doesn't hurt to ask."

Trent's smile grew wider, his teeth strikingly white

against his tanned face. "Ladies, I'm beyond flattered. But I am for Maddie's eyes only," he said, cupping her chin and turning her face up toward him. She held her breath or maybe just plain forgot to breathe. Then he slowly leaned in, his lips brushing hers, soft and sweet.

Oh, he is so worth the money...

Her aunts let out a collective sigh. Or maybe that was her.

"Don't let the WD-40 Effect win, dear. He's too good to let slip away."

Marie's comment snapped her brain back to normal functioning, and she pulled away from Trent. Maddie had thought she could escape those kinds of remarks from her family, but even with a date on her arm, her family still seemed to doubt she wasn't somehow cursed.

"I'll do my best," she said, forcing a smile.

"This should help." Her aunt Lois pulled out what looked to be some kind of bright pink origami and held it out to her.

Maddie looked at it, but made no move to take it. "What's that?"

"It's a duct tape bracelet. We made it for you."

She glanced at Trent who looked as confused as she felt. She hated to ask, but... "Okay. Um...*why*?"

Lois gave her a full-wattage dentures grin. "Duct tape is the opposite of WD-40. We thought you should wear it for good luck. Isn't that clever? We should have done this years ago after that nice fireman you dated went back to his old girlfriend."

Maddie closed her eyes. *The family insanity continues...*

"Oh, look," Trent said, "the groom's family is going to

say a few words now."

With relief, Maddie opened her eyes and looked to where a piano had been stationed. Michael's father already had the microphone and was thanking friends and family for coming to the party. Aunt Marie, whose hearing was on a downhill slope, made a mad dash to the front. Her aunt Lois was about to follow but not before taking Maddie's hand, placing the bracelet in her palm, and squeezing her fingers closed around it.

"Wear it in good health, dear," she whispered before leaving.

Maddie looked at Trent. "Do you believe what I'm dealing with here?"

"Only because I saw it with my own eyes." He surprised her when he took her hand in his and kissed the back of it. "But I'd still take your family over mine any day. Come on. Let's go join the others."

She nodded, feeling surprisingly good-humored. Even if bringing a date to Louise's wedding wasn't deflecting talk about her being cursed, she was still glad Trent was here with her. She didn't think he could be such a comfort and support, but she didn't know how she'd manage through this evening and the rest of the week if it wasn't for him.

Louise and Michael were holding hands as Michael's father passed the microphone to his wife. "We're so delighted you all could come ahead of the wedding and share in our joy of Michael and Louise's happiness," she told everyone. "We hope you enjoy the rest of the festivities we have planned, too. But before we drink to our son and future daughter-in-law, could we have the maid of honor come forward to lead us in a toast?"

Maddie froze as all eyes turned toward her.

"Oh, crikey," she murmured. "A little heads-up would have been nice."

"Come on, sweetheart," Michael's mom said. "Come say a few words for Louise and Michael."

Trent nudged her forward. "You can do this. For Louise," he whispered in her ear.

She ignored the little shiver that went down her neck from Trent's closeness and took a deep breath. He was right. Although she wasn't prepared to speak—at least not until the wedding day—she could say what was in her heart. About the happiness and love Louise had found. And what she hoped to find for herself someday.

Maddie gave a slight smile as she took the microphone and tried to combat the butterflies growing in her stomach. "Um, hi," she said awkwardly. "I just wanted to say that although I can't speak from experience, I do know relationships are hard work. And I can see with Louise and Michael that when you find the right person, that work becomes easy, because you have two people working together toward the same goal. I'm so proud of Louise for never settling." She glanced over at Louise, whose smile broadened in approval. "And I'm proud of Michael for realizing how special my sister is and for never letting her go."

Maddie took a glass of champagne that was sitting on the piano for her and raised it in the air. The crowd mimicked her action. "To Louise and Michael. Love each other deeply and hold on to each other above everything else."

She drank deeply as her gaze clouded with tears. She wished someone would hold on to her. Men unfortunately had no problem letting her go. Even her own father. But she had a strong feeling in her heart that Louise would not suffer that fate with Michael.

The band began to play "When I Fall in Love" and everything seemed to hit her at once. How ridiculously sad her own life had become. She couldn't find a job or a date—or at least, she couldn't find a date without paying for one. She placed the empty flute down and made her way through the crowd of dancers. Her mind was in such a cloud she hadn't realized she had walked right past Trent.

He took hold of her arm, stopping her. "Hey, I believe you promised me this dance. And I lead."

"There will be others," she said, shaking her head. She was hardly in the mood to dance. All she wanted to do was go back to the room and bury herself under the covers. Possibly with a pint of Chunky Monkey.

He looked directly into her eyes, his face right above hers. "As your devoted wedding date, I have to insist. Plus, Louise is watching us, probably wondering why we aren't out on the dance floor with them."

Weariness overtook her, and she nodded. He was right. At least somebody was able to keep the charade going. Trent was definitely all business and played his part well, which made it even harder to go right back into his arms so soon after their kiss. It only made her want things that would never be for real.

As soon as their feet touched the patio, he placed her hand on his shoulder then slid his own to her waist. He was silent for a while, which she was grateful for because it gave her time to regulate her breathing. His nearness was so overwhelming. And for a moment she felt like she was floating. She wondered if her legs had even moved yet.

"Pretty speech," he finally commented, breaking her out of her jumbled up thoughts.

His tone sounded almost mocking, so she looked up to judge his expression. But his face was blank. "Thanks. I think."

"You're welcome. If you meant what you said."

"Why wouldn't I wish my sister all the happiness in the world?"

"I wondered if you meant what you said about them holding on to each other above everything else."

"Of course. Everything else is fleeting, but love lasts forever."

"Sure it does."

She stopped and stared at him in disbelief. "You sound cynical about love. You can't be cynical. *I'm* the one who should be cynical."

Trent pasted on a polite smile when people glanced over at them, unmoving on the dance floor. "Your feet seemed to have stopped moving, *honey*. If you don't give me at least one hip sway, I'm going to be forced to dip you. And PS, I have every right to be cynical."

"That makes no sense whatsoever."

"Dipping you or being cynical?"

"Both."

"All right. You asked for it." And then she felt herself go backward.

He swung her up again just as fast, and a rush of excitement went through her. "At least you warned me," she said with a laugh, brushing at her hair that got caught in her lip gloss.

His eyes gleamed with humor. "Next time you won't be

so lucky."

"Ha, next time I'll be prepared. I know your moves now."

He leaned in and brought his face close to hers. "Not all of them, honey," he whispered in her ear.

A thrill shot up her spine, and she nearly stumbled.

"Are you feeling better?" he asked suddenly.

"You mean now that all the blood has rushed back to my feet again?"

He chuckled. "Yes, that, and in general. You seemed a bit out of it after you toasted the bride and groom."

"Actually, I am feeling better. Thanks for asking me to dance."

"What are fake boyfriends for?"

She smiled. "Well, this fake girlfriend hasn't dated anyone for real this nice in a long time and appreciates it."

Trent stepped back, closing his warm fingers over hers, and twirled her under his arm. "You're welcome," he said, drawing her in to his chest again. "I'm glad I officially broke my bad-boy image to you."

"Sorry, pal. The jury is still out on that, I'm afraid."

"Damn, you are one hard woman, Maddie McCarthy. But I do like a challenge."

"And cheerleaders apparently," she quipped.

"That does it." He dipped her again and when he pulled her back up, they were both laughing.

Louise elbowed her out of the blue. "Hey, I don't think you guys are allowed to have more fun than the engaged couple," she teased, still dancing with Michael.

Maddie felt her cheeks go hot. She *was* having fun. She couldn't remember the last time she had really let go and enjoyed herself with a man like that. Even with his cynical commentary on love, she really was enjoying Trent's company.

Just remember it's his job to be charming.

"Trent, promise me you'll dance like that with me on my wedding day," Louise said with a wink.

"I'll definitely save you a dip. Start practicing your yoga moves now."

Louise grinned. "You bet I will."

Trent took Maddie's hand and twirled her around. She marveled at how such a brawny kind of guy could move so fluidly. "Louise may need to practice but you sure don't. Did Match Made Easy require you to take dance lessons before they'd hire you?" she asked a little out of breath.

"No." Just like that the humor left his face.

As soon as the song ended, he led her to the bar, and she became a little disconcerted when he immediately handed her a Chardonnay. "How did you know that's what I wanted to drink?" she asked.

"It's what you drank when I met your mom. And when we went out to dinner that night." He frowned. "I'm sorry. I shouldn't have assumed."

"No, you shouldn't have." She took the wine from his hand and took a healthy sip. It was crisp and tart with just a hint of sweetness. "But in this case, you'd be right. It's exactly what I wanted. You're very good at what you do. I suppose that's why you're paid the big bucks."

"Big bucks? Oh, right. What can I say, I'm a professional," he said flatly. He clinked her glass with his own glass of Scotch, but didn't drink any of it. Instead, he scanned the yard, looking distracted.

Something had definitely changed with him, and she

wondered what she'd said to affect his mood.

The bar started to get crowded, so they took their drinks and walked down the stone path to the bay. There was a bench facing the water surrounded by white and pink flowering landscaping. Maddie immediately sat down, already exhausted and perfectly happy to stay there until the sun set, but she knew she couldn't hide from her family all night.

Trent sat down beside her, continuing to stare off into the distance. His mouth was tight and grim. She knew that look well. If they were dating for real, she would have assumed it meant he was trying to come up with a way to break up with her.

"So…how 'bout those Red Sox," she said.

The beginning of a smile tipped the corners of his mouth. "I'm a football guy, remember?"

"Football, baseball, it's all the same."

He clutched his heart, pretending to be wounded. "For your information, it is *not* all the same. Football is the ultimate American sport. A Sunday tradition. All players are involved in one play and playoff games actually mean something. Plus, football players play in all weather, not like those hypersensitive baseball pansies."

"Okay, okay. Sheesh. I obviously struck a nerve. I'll have to watch a game sometime."

"Damn straight. In fact, I'll personally take you to a Patriots game."

She stilled. "You will?"

"Absolutely. I own season tickets."

Maddie looked down at her wineglass and banked down the little bubble of joy that sprung up at his suggestion. What was she even remotely excited about? He didn't really mean it. Besides, football season wasn't for months, and in a few days they would probably never see each other again once his contract was fulfilled.

"This is some engagement party," Trent said, motioning with his Scotch glass. "Your sister is going to be one rich bride."

Maddie narrowed her eyes. "That's not why she's marrying Michael."

He paused a beat. "No, I guess not. She doesn't seem the type."

"She isn't the type. She's the sweetest, kindest person ever. And if Michael lost all his money tomorrow, Louise would still have him."

"Michael is very lucky then."

The sadness in his tone got her attention. She looked at him closely, seeing a hardened shell around him for reasons that went beyond Louise and Michael's upcoming marriage. "Trent, why don't you like weddings?"

He seemed startled for a moment then carefully schooled his expression. "What's to like about them?"

"Nuh-uh. Answer my question first."

He let a few moments pass, seeming to mull it over. Then he finally answered, "I was engaged."

Not the answer she expected. "You were? What happened?"

"Nothing happened as you can guess from my lack of wife. She got cold feet the day before the wedding. Exactly five days after I dropped out of the NFL draft. I guess I lost my appeal once I stopped playing football. The real kicker was that she called my parents to apologize before she called me. Wouldn't want to fall too far under the good graces of the Montgomery family," he said in a bitter tone.

He blew out a breath as if he had unloaded a ton of weight from his chest. "To answer your question from before, my fiancée made me take dance lessons for the wedding that never was. Glad they finally came to some use."

Maddie just sat there. Every word that popped into her head seemed trivial and cliché, so she didn't say anything for several moments. For a man to still be dead set against weddings after all this time, it would seem to matter very much. No wonder he wasn't involved with anyone seriously and worked as an escort. The job protected him from getting too close.

"I'm sorry, Trent."

"Looking back on it now, she probably did us both a favor. We were both naive and self-centered. Her leaving me made me take stock of my priorities and what's really important. I decided to open up a gym but knew I wanted it to be more than just a superficial business. I wanted it to make a difference mentally *and* physically to people."

"How so?"

"One of the things I want to start up in my gyms is a youth center for kids. Once I get some money saved, that is, and pay off my bank loan. I'd like some of the young men who don't have role models at home to be able to find them at my gym. Sports, working out, can give them a purpose. Coaches can have a wonderful influence on kids like that. I should know. I had a great one in college. It's important those kids know they're worth more than how much they can lift or how far they can throw a ball."

"That does sound wonderful."

"It will be as long as I can pay off my line of credit next

month."

"Do you think you will?"

He thought about it for a second but wouldn't meet her gaze. "Yeah. I have something on the back burner that looks as if it should work. At least, I hope it does. My business—my work—is what I've decided to give my heart to instead of a person."

Tenderness washed over her, and she wove her arm through his to comfort him. "Your fiancée did a horrible thing. But that doesn't mean you have to give up on love and weddings and happily-ever-afters."

"And *you* haven't?"

"Well…"

She went speechless.

It wasn't as if she'd given up on them *in general*. She believed in all that forever love stuff for her sister. She just didn't see it in her own future.

"That's what I thought," he said, standing and offering her his hand. "We should get back to the party. You're not paying me to talk."

She put her hand in his and allowed him to pull her up. "You're not a bad guy," she blurted.

His brows lifted. "Gee, thanks?"

"I mean, I thought you were. Back in high school. Now I know I misjudged you."

"You're just being nice because you feel sorry for me for being jilted."

"Not at all. She was stupid to leave you. "

"Really?"

"Of course. I don't see why she would want you more if you played professionally. Football is way overrated."

His face fell. "I hope that sacrilegious statement was not intended to cheer me up."

"Sorry," she said, holding in a laugh. "Not a football fan, remember?"

"I'll make you one soon enough." He gave her a long smoldering look before turning and leading her up the path. "Just wait and see."

"I'd like to see you try," she murmured.

Unfortunately, with the way her feelings toward Trent were changing, he wouldn't need to work too hard to persuade her.

"It was a wonderful evening thanks to you," Louise said, wrapping her arms around Maddie's middle and squeezing her like a hungry python.

"I…didn't…do anything," she wheezed out.

Louise pulled back with a laugh. "Of course you did! The lovely impromptu speech you gave brought tears to my eyes. And well, just the fact that you were having such a good time made me happy, too. I'm the one getting married, but I so wanted us to celebrate it together."

"Me, too." Maddie turned her head and brushed away a tear with her finger. All she wanted was this day to be special for Louise. No talk of curses. Just joy and dreams for the future. And thanks to Trent's convincing portrayal of devoted boyfriend, she was able to pull that feat off.

So far, anyway.

As if her just thinking about him summoned him, Trent appeared, holding a corsage out to her sister. "The caterers were going to toss this, but I thought you might want to save it in some mementos book or something."

"Oh, I had forgotten I'd taken it off to dance," Louise said, sliding it back on her wrist. "You are so sweet and thoughtful to think of that." Smiling, she leaned in and kissed him on the cheek. "Thank you so much."

"You're welcome," he told her then shot a quick wink at Maddie.

"Maddie, this guy is a treasure," she said, patting his arm affectionately. "He fits in with our family so well. I feel like you've been with him forever."

Maddie resisted an eye roll. "It kind of feels like forever to me, too."

Trent grinned, wrapping an arm around her and pulling her in close. "Forever and ever, amen," he said low in her ear.

A small shiver raced down her spine as his breath tickled her earlobe. Because of that she felt a small urge to lean in and get closer, but forced herself to pull away. "Um, it's getting late, darling, and I'm sure Louise would like to spend more time with her fiancé before going to bed."

Trent's eyes seemed to glimmer at the mention of the word bed. He suddenly yawned and gave an unnatural stretch. "You know, we should hit the hay, too, honey."

Maddie frowned, suddenly remembering they were sharing a room and, more importantly, a bed together. "You know…on second thought, it's not that late. Maybe Louise and Michael want to get together for a game of cards?"

Louise made a face. "Cards?"

"You like board games instead? How about Monopoly?"

"Monopoly? That could take all night," Louise complained.

"Monopoly it is then!" Maddie pivoted, about to make

her way to the main house, but Trent grabbed her hand.

"Louise looks wiped, darling. Save all this newfound energy for when we get back to our room," he said with a grin, pulling her toward the guest house instead. "Good night, Louise."

Louise giggled. "Good night, you two. See you for the festivities tomorrow."

Maddie bit her tongue the entire four minute walk to their room, but once they were inside with the door tightly closed behind her, she thwacked Trent in the chest. "You're not following my lead at all."

"Honey, you ever want to lead a bunch of seniors in a canasta match, I'll follow your so-called lead 100 percent. But as it turns out, it's one in the morning and we're at a twenty-something's engagement party. I needed to take control of the reins."

He jerked himself away from the door and began loosening his tie. As annoyed as she was, Maddie had to admit, he had a gorgeous throat. He shrugged out of his suit jacket then began unbuttoning his shirt. If she allowed his fingers to continue south much longer, she was sure she'd be admiring other parts of him as well, which was starting to make her feel…edgy.

She hesitated one brief second then held up her hand like a crossing guard. "Halt!" she blurted.

Trent paused and quirked an eyebrow. "Halt?"

"Um, yes." She swallowed. "Don't you think you should change in, um, private?"

"No."

She huffed out a breath. Of course he wouldn't. Women paid top dollar to drape a body like his over their arm at various functions. He probably even thought he was giving her an added unpaid treat of some sort, thinking the poor girl who had to hire a wedding date hadn't gotten any in a while and could use a cheap thrill. Well. That may be true, but she still didn't appreciate it.

"I *do* think you should change in private. You don't see me ripping off my clothes in front of *you*, now do you?"

He gave a deep fake sigh. "Sadly, no."

The man was impossible, giving her mixed signals again. He wasn't supposed to be funny and charming in private, only in front of others. What he was getting paid to do. She couldn't deal with his hot body, either. Her resistance was particularly low tonight, and she was afraid that if he did make one small move on her she'd pounce on him like a ninja.

"What do you want to do about the sleeping arrangements?" she asked, trying to control the shaking in her voice.

"I can see the wheels spinning in your head," he remarked with a grin. "Are you seriously so afraid to be near me that you can't share a bed for sleeping purposes only?"

Maybe.

She brushed a wild curl out of her face. "Of course not. I was only giving you the option in case you felt uncomfortable sharing a bed with *me*."

Trent flopped down on the bed, placing his hands behind his head. "Totally comfortable here."

Her shoulders wilted. "Oh…good. Me, too. Totally comfortable about the whole situation."

He crossed his ankles and grinned, looking completely at ease with his half nakedness and rock-hard body.

Damn him.

She marched over to her suitcase and dragged it into the bathroom with her. After she finished changing and brushed her teeth, she cracked open the door. The bedroom was pitch black. Trent must have fallen asleep. Perfect.

She tiptoed over to the bed and slid under the covers, carefully trying to not shift the mattress. Once she was settled, she let out a quiet breath and willed her body to relax.

"Maddie," Trent whispered, disrupting the silence.

She tensed. "Yes?"

"Are you mad at me?"

She almost laughed. "No. Not anymore."

She couldn't see her hand in front of her face but could tell that Trent had turned and was staring at her. "Look, I didn't mean to upset you earlier. To be honest, it is awkward for me to be sharing a bed with an attractive woman and not be…involved with her."

"I'm attractive? I mean, you're uncomfortable?"

"But I want to assure you that I'm 100 percent the professional. Your virtue is perfectly safe with me."

Safe virtue. Just what I need. Oh, joy. "Thanks," she muttered. She was grateful for the cover of darkness because she was sure all animation had left her face. Of course "Fatty Maddie" was safe from any of his advances. How could she think otherwise?

"Are we good now?" he asked.

Even though she was buzzing with lust and confusion, she answered, "Yeah, we're good. Good night, Trent."

"Do you want Ryan back?"

She was about to turn on her side, but his abrupt question held her frozen. "What?"

"The best man. Do you want him back?"

Do I?

"No. I may appear desperate but I'm not that desperate."

He chuckled. "Good. Because you deserve better."

The room went silent for several beats as she thought about how to respond to such a statement. She did deserve better—deep in her heart she knew that—but it was nice to hear someone like Trent think so, too.

"Good night, Maddie," he said softly, and she felt the bed rustle until he got comfortable.

"Good night," she answered, holding in a sigh.

Because she had a feeling her night was going to be anything but good.

Chapter Eight

Trent was dreaming.

And what a friggin' dream. It ranked right up there with winning the Super Bowl against the Dallas Cowboys where Tony Romo went out of his way to shake his hand. Yeah, that was pretty sweet. But this dream…

This dream was *much* better. He was holding something soft and sweet-smelling. An angel. All gold haloed and lovely. Her closeness was like a drug, making his body feel heavy and warm. He buried his face into her hair and wanted to stay like that forever.

However, forever was short-lived when something smacked him in the face. He woke, blinking up at the bedroom ceiling.

"What the hell?" he said groggily, holding his cheek where there was a sudden and very painful stinging sensation.

"You took the words right out of my mouth, you— you—"

He raised a hand, stopping Maddie from finishing what he could only imagine was a less than flattering adjective. So much for his angel.

"What are you all worked up about?" he asked warily.

"This," she spat, motioning to the small space where she sat and he lay, "is what I call taking advantage." Glaring, she looked all flustered and—Lord-don't-put-him-in-more-hot-water-than-he-already-was—sexy with her blond curls bouncing with each word she sputtered. "And you can kindly remove your hand now, too."

He glanced down and blinked. Then, with as much remorse as he could muster, he carefully slid his hand out from underneath her butt.

"Good grief, do you even have any clothes on?" She jerked back the covers before he could answer. He couldn't tell if it was relief or disappointment on her face when she saw his plaid boxers. "You were supposed to stay on your side of the bed."

He yanked back the covers, his own anger growing. "How do you know I didn't? You could have come over to *my* side of the bed, honey. I don't know why you're even upset. So maybe I copped a feel in my sleep. It's not my fault. I'm a man. We're programmed that way," he huffed. "I'll sleep in the bathtub tonight, okay?"

Maddie pressed a hand to her eyes and sighed. "No. You don't have to do that. I know nothing happened. I don't know why I'm overreacting. I think this wedding is just getting to me. I'm sorry."

"It's okay," he grumbled. "Could have done without the slap in the face wake-up call, though."

"I said I was sorry. It's bad enough that we have to share

a bed. But I wasn't expecting to wake up together like a twisted pretzel on top of everything."

She crossed her arms over her chest, and his gaze dipped to finally take in what she wore to bed. It had been late last night and the lights were off by the time she climbed onto her side. He smiled at her T-shirt covered in little sheep. She probably thought a shirt like that wouldn't inspire nefarious thoughts, but she'd underestimated the mind of a healthy, single, heterosexual man. And the power she apparently had over him.

"I understand," he said, nodding. "If it makes you feel better, you can touch me all you want when you're sleeping."

The warmth of her laughter heated his insides. "Thanks so much."

Silence eventually grew between them. "So...do you want to?" he asked, watching for her reaction.

"Want to what?"

"Touch me."

She bit her lip, those soft, plump lips that drove him crazy just looking at them. "Trent, I— It's not about what I want. I thought we're keeping this professional, so we don't muck up our working relationship, right?"

Trent would have agreed with her wholeheartedly as he'd done before. But it was the doubt in her tone and expression that had him ignoring her question and taking what he'd been denying himself for too long.

He reached up and cupped her chin. "Right now, you can consider me off the clock," he whispered, before his mouth met hers. No more sweet and gentle. This time he showed her all fire and heat. How crazy she was making him even in her sheep nightshirt.

She slipped her arms around his neck, and he pulled her closer. "Maddie," he groaned against her lips.

He had dated plenty of women. Came close to being married. But never had he felt this overpowering need that went beyond mere physical attraction. Almost as if he'd combust if he had to spend one single moment away from her. He wondered if she felt the same, would want to continue dating after…after the wedding.

The wedding she'd hired him to attend with her.

Oh crap. Maddie believed he worked for Match Made Easy. He needed to tell her the truth. If this thing between them was going to go anywhere, he couldn't continue lying to her. He jerked back as that thought struck him.

She blinked at him all heavy lidded with passion, and he suddenly had second thoughts about pulling away. "Is there a problem?" she asked.

Problem? Would she hate him for not telling her the truth about his cousin's business from the beginning? Would she file a complaint against Match Made Easy once she learned he wasn't an escort? Would she even believe he really was starting to have feelings for her?

He shook his head. "No problem. I just realized what time it is. We, uh, need to get ready for the festivities. Can't have the maid of honor absent."

"Uh. That's right. I forgot about the *festivities.*"

Trent drew in a breath and rolled off of her, knowing it was best even if it killed him to do so. Before anything went further between them, he'd have to find a way to explain the situation to her, give her the honesty that he'd come to require in any relationship.

Relationship?

He almost laughed. Maybe all those wedding speeches had gone to his head, or maybe he sensed in Maddie the same trust issues he'd been holding on to. Either way, he was starting to believe there could be something there worth taking a leap of faith. Something unconditional.

Maddie shifted onto her side, resting her cheek in her hand. "Michael's mom is actually flying in the head chef from the Ritz Carlton in New York to give us all a personal cooking demonstration. What are the men scheduled to do?"

"Golf." He wiggled his eyebrows. "My next-best sport."

She laughed. "Figures. Try not to upstage my future brother in-law."

"Can't promise that. Blame my competitive streak."

His phone's text message alert went off. Maddie grabbed his phone off the side table and frowned as she handed it to him. "It's from Kennedy," she said stiffly.

Well...that timing could have been better.

"Is she checking in?" she asked, making her way to the bathroom.

He scanned the text. "No, she can't find Bella's leash," he murmured.

She stopped at the doorway and arched a brow. "Your boss is watching your dog for you?"

"Uh, yeah. She's...she's really good like that." He swallowed and pointed to his phone. "You go ahead and shower. I'm going to respond to Kennedy and make sure my dog is still alive."

Her brows knit in confusion but she turned into the bathroom, the door closing behind her.

That was awkward. Trent quietly let out a breath. He couldn't continue deceiving Maddie like this. She was starting to mean something to him. He was going to have to tell his cousin that things had changed, and the whole charade was over.

And pray everything worked out for both of them.

Maddie had been in a few large-scale restaurants in her day, but she still couldn't keep her jaw from dropping at the spacious — and immaculate — kitchen of the main house. Even with twenty women crowding around the granite island where Chef Dean was showing the proper technique of deglazing, there wasn't a bad seat to be had.

"I would pay close attention, Maddie," Veronica whispered. "Maybe you'll pick up something that'll help you get a job."

Maddie glared at her. "Graduated with honors from culinary school, thank you very much."

Her cousin snorted. "A lot of good it did."

That did it. Maddie threw the dish towel that was resting on her shoulder down on the counter. Little did Veronica know but she was seconds away from a face full of flour.

Louise rushed over to them, wedging her body between them. "Isn't this fun, guys?" Her smile was bright albeit nervous. "I always wanted to learn how to make" — she frowned in the direction of the stove — "whatever he's making."

Maddie chuckled. Her sister was not a cook, although it would seem that wasn't a quality she'd really be utilizing in Michael's family, anyway.

"It's a real hoot," her cousin said, checking her watch. "But when is this demo going to be over? I was hoping to get a little sun today before my boyfriend arrives."

Louise shrugged. "I'm not sure. I think he's going to show us another main entrée and a dessert still."

Aunt Marie turned to them with a finger raised against her lips. "Shhh!"

Maddie exchanged a smile with her sister. "Uh-oh. We've officially been *shhhed*," she said to Louise.

They giggled like they were in high school. But the thought of high school only reminded her of Trent. What was really going on between them? She'd thought she'd hired him for a simple job as her wedding date. Only, the lines were kind of blurred from what she thought was pretend and what was now resembling reality. With her track record she hated to get her hopes up, but Trent knew the pain of being left behind. Surely he wouldn't be able to walk away from her so easily after the wedding was over—curse or no stupid curse. But she couldn't be sure.

Louise snagged a piece of chicken from the plate being passed around. "How's your room?" she asked with a knowing grin.

Maddie shrugged. "Fine."

"Fine? My future mother-in-law wanted to place Michael's grandma in that room. But I fought for you, since it's the most private," she said, overpronouncing the word private. "Please tell me it's more than just *fine* and you two are getting some quality alone time together. I want you guys to feel as though you're on a romantic getaway."

Well, this morning felt like a romantic getaway. Sort of. The way Trent had passionately kissed her made her toes curl like party favors. He had wanted her. There was no mistaking that. Then he received that text from Kennedy, and he started to act weird. Or maybe she acted weird, which made *him* act weird. Ugh. Maybe she was overthinking this.

"Thanks," she said, pulling Louise into a hug. "Trent and I are having a lovely time."

"I'm so glad. You know, Trent's really different from other guys you dated. "

You're telling me. Technically they weren't even dating… or were they? The way he kissed sure made her feel that way.

A dull throb began to bloom in her head. She reached up and applied pressure with her fingers, wishing—like everything else in her life—she could WD-40 it away.

Chef Dean clasped his hands together and looked at the group expectantly. "Now I think it's time for some volunteers. How about the chatty madame to my left?" he said, with a wave of his hand in Maddie's direction.

Maddie's face heated. "Oh. Uh, sure." Feeling like she'd been singled out by a teacher in school for chewing gum, she slowly slid off her stool. She made her way around the island and stood next to Chef.

"And perhaps you?" he asked Veronica.

Veronica grabbed her cheeks as if she had beat out Meryl Streep for an Academy Award. "Oh, thank you. I'd love to. You can call me Vonnie."

Maddie pursed her lips. *Puh-leeeeze.* Wasn't this the same woman who just asked when she could leave? And now she was all gooey eyes and eyelash flutters.

"Okay, ladies," Chef Dean explained, "we are going to attempt to make a delicious beef stir-fry that can easily be whipped up when you come home from a hard day's work."

Veronica cast a meaningful glance at Maddie. "What if

you don't have a job?"

Chef Dean's brows knit together. "Uh, then you can make it anytime you are hungry."

Maddie kept silent, refusing to be baited. This was not going to be about her or her cousin. She'd rise above her dislike for Louise's sake. "What would you like me to do?" she asked him.

"Ah. I want you to slice the vegetables like I demonstrated, and in the meantime, Vonnie here will sauté the strips of tenderloin."

Veronica's face lit up. "Isn't that cute? You're going to be *my* sous chef, Maddie."

Maddie gave her a tight-lipped smile. "Give me the knife," she said to the chef through clenched teeth.

"Uh…" Louise raised her hand. "Maybe weapons aren't such a good thing to have here."

Chef Dean let out a hearty laugh. "They're not weapons, my dear. Used the way I demonstrated, they are precious equipment used to create extraordinary culinary taste experiences."

Louise worried her lip. "Is that before or after someone dies?"

"Wow, somebody is morbid," Michael's mother commented, wrinkling her nose.

"Don't worry," Maddie said, taking the knife from Chef Dean. "I'm a professional, remember?"

"I like this one's attitude," Chef Dean said. "First rule in the kitchen is to not be intimidated by the kitchen. Yes?"

"Yes." Maddie grabbed a yellow bell pepper and began slicing it in perfect julienne strips. She may not have a job to use her skills, but she hadn't forgotten them. Chef Dean patted her on the shoulder when she was finished and gave her an approving smile.

Take that, Veronica!

Veronica frowned at the plate of uncooked meat. "Does it always look so…dead?"

That remark was rewarded by several chuckles from the audience of women. Chef Dean cleared his throat. "If you think it looks dead now, wait until you drop it into the pan of hot oil."

"Do I, uh, have to touch it?" she asked.

Maddie picked up a pair of tongs and held them out to her. "Use these."

Chef Dean handed her a white onion. "You seem very comfortable working in a kitchen," he commented to her.

"I am." Maddie smiled. "I have some restaurant experience at the Red Tomato but things didn't work out and they cut their staff." *Thanks to the no good rat best man.* "I'm looking for another job."

"Send your resume to me, and I'll see what I can do for you."

She looked up into his eyes to judge if he was serious. "Really? Thank you so much. That would be great."

"Oh, Maddie," Louise exclaimed, "a new boyfriend and now a possible new job! I'm so excited for you."

Maddie tried to control a squeal. Things really were changing for her. At least in the job aspect of her life. Her eyes began to water, and it had nothing to do with the onion she was slicing.

Veronica held the strip of beef between the tongs like it was some animal carcass she found on the side of the road. "What do I do now?"

"The oil is bubbling, so now lay it gently in the pan," Chef told her.

Following directions or advice was never one of her cousin's strong points, so it wasn't surprising to Maddie when Veronica ended up flinging the meat away from her instead. The steak landed with a loud *splat* as hot oil splashed out of the pan. Some of the women screamed, afraid to be hit, and her aunts and Chef Dean jumped out of the way. Someone bumped her shoulder, and the knife slipped.

A stinging sensation registered. Maddie looked down at her hand. Blood began to trickle down and cover her thumb.

"So not good," she heard herself say. Her mouth went dry. She began perspiring.

Did somebody turn off the AC?

Voices mingled in the background. Her mom grabbed her arm and wrapped it up in a towel. She was asking her questions, but Maddie could only stare at the blood that started to seep through the material. The room swayed a few times.

And then it went black.

Trent took his time, lined up the shot, and gave the ball a gentle tap. The ball slowly rotated along the green and then…popped right into the hole. *Yes.*

Michael shook his head but grinned. "I'm glad we're playing Best Ball, and you're on my team."

Trent bent down to retrieve his ball with a grin on his face. He was glad he was on Michael's team, too, and not stuck with that tool, Ryan. Despite being apart from Maddie,

Trent was actually enjoying himself—just as much for the company as it was the sport. Louise's fiancé was a pretty cool guy—for a billionaire. Michael seemed to take to Trent as well, so much so that Trent felt comfortable enough plugging Kennedy's company to him. He seemed genuinely interested, but that didn't mean Trent felt any less guilty for trying to score his cousin some serious advertising dibs at Fenway Park come baseball season. But a promise was a promise.

Trent tucked his putter back into his bag and removed his glove as Michael opened up the cooler.

"What's your secret?" asked Michael, handing him a beer.

"Practice." That was the truth. He'd had plenty of it growing up with the kind of country club circles his parents tried to infiltrate.

Michael gave him a shrewd look. "Does that relate to women as well?"

He raised the bottle to his lips and paused. "What do you mean?"

Michael grimaced. "Hell. I don't know what I mean." He rubbed the back of his neck and tried again. "It's just that you and Maddie seem like you have a good thing going."

"You think? Er, I mean, yeah, we do." *Or at least, we could.* Unfortunately, Maddie didn't seem like she put a whole lot of stock into her own self-worth or into men in general, but he was hoping to change all that. If she gave him the chance.

"You guys have something I thought I had," Michael said. "But now, in two days, Louise and I are going to be married, and she's acting as if we're mild acquaintances. I don't get it."

"Maybe she's uncomfortable around your parents. Or it could be stress."

Michael shrugged as if Trent's words made no difference. "Something's off."

"I wouldn't worry about it, man. Maddie assured me that Louise has no doubts about her feelings for you."

Michael looked over, letting out a relieved smile. "Thanks. That's good to hear."

Trent clapped him on the back. "Anytime."

"Hey, no BS. I'll definitely give this Kennedy Pepperdine a call for you. I might be able to squeeze in an ad slot for her at a reasonable rate."

Trent was about to thank him when Michael's cell phone went off. Retrieving it from his pocket, Michael slid his finger over the screen then raised it up to his ear. "Hey, we were just talking about you, honey," he said, winking at Trent.

Michael turned away, lowering his voice. "Okay, relax. I'll let him know. Okay. Love you, too." He switched off his phone then stared at Trent for a moment, looking as if he had to collect his thoughts.

"Is Louise okay?"

"Uh, yeah. Louise is fine. But there was a little accident in the kitchen today. Maddie cut herself."

Nausea began to stir in his stomach. "Cut herself? How bad?"

"I don't know." Michael's face went grim. "She's in the ER right now."

Chapter Nine

"Mom, please. I'm fine. Just sign me out already." Maddie waved away her mom's fussing with her good hand and attempted to sit up from the hospital bed. "It's embarrassing enough that they made me put on this drafty hospital gown."

Her mom folded her arms. "You have nothing to be embarrassed about. Lots of people don't care for the sight of blood."

"And faint and hit their heads on trashcans?"

"Well, it was a good thing it was there. It broke your fall."

Maddie's head began to throb again, so she sat back on the bed. "Yeah, lucky me," she grumbled.

"There, there," her mom said, stroking her hair. "You'll feel better once Louise brings you your Diet Coke."

Maddie sighed, suddenly feeling pathetic and just a little bit sorry for herself. Who knows what Chef Dean thought of her little fainting episode? And now she'd gone and ruined her sister's pre-wedding activity. "Mom, you don't think I'm cursed, do you?"

Her mom laughed. "Not at all."

"Are you sure? I mean, I'm starting to have my doubts."

"There is no curse, dear."

"I know that. Deep down inside I do know that. But... maybe there's a wee bit of truth to it."

"Don't be silly. Look at you. Despite Veronica's carelessness, you have all your fingers. Plus, Chef Dean will still try and get you a job, which means soon you'll be back in your own apartment. And of course, let's not forget about Trent."

Maddie frowned. "What about Trent?"

"I'm so glad you finally met someone like him. I was getting worried. It gets harder and harder to meet nice men the older you get."

It gets harder the more cursed you are, too, but knowing that wouldn't go over well, she didn't bother mentioning it. "Let's not get carried away here. I'm only thirty."

"Thirty-one in September," her mom reminded her, wagging a finger.

Her spirits sank even lower. She should have told Louise to skip the diet soda. She was going to need the real sugar stuff. Maybe a doughnut, too, since she missed having any food at the cooking demonstration.

"What if I didn't have Trent?" she blurted.

Her mom smiled at her as if she thought Maddie were slow-witted. "But you do have Trent."

"Right, but what if he and I suddenly broke up? Would you think I was cursed then?"

Her mom chuckled. "Honey, you must have hit your

head a lot harder than you thought. You're talking nonsense. Trent seems like the kind of guy who will stick. Don't be so negative."

"Yeah. Maybe." But she couldn't help feeling that once the wedding was over and his services were paid for, there wouldn't be much reason for Trent to remain in her life. Sure, he was attracted to her. That much she could tell, but after that… His cynicism toward love was apparent. He certainly didn't seem like the type who was looking for a serious relationship. At least, he gave her no impression that he even considered it. He had to be a paid escort for a simple reason: he enjoyed women at an arm's length. So why get her hopes up? It would only lead to devastation.

Louise stuck her head in the door. "Hey, Maddie. Are you decent?"

"What kind of question is that?" she huffed. "And you better have my diet soda."

Her sister grinned. "Don't worry. I have your soda and something *much* better."

Maddie hoped she meant a ham sandwich, but then her heart turned over when she saw Trent storm in behind her. Even with his eyes wide with concern and his hair stuck up in tufts, he looked like a Greek Adonis.

She took in a sharp breath. "Trent, you came."

"Of course he would come," her mother said, looking appalled she would even question such a thing. "Louise called Michael to let him know right away."

"Yes, of course I came," he said gruffly. "Now what the hell happened?"

Maddie swallowed at his dark mood. Now probably wasn't the best time to mention that he needed to work on his bedside manner. She lifted her bandaged hand. "Just a few stitches."

"She bumped her head, too," Louise supplied. "But no concussion, thank goodness."

Trent strode over and stopped in front of her. The bigness of him and his charged emotion filled every space in the room. She merely sat tongue-tied as he brought his hands up and inspected her head with the gentleness of a butterfly. After a moment or two, he dropped his arms to the side and sat down next to her. "All I heard was that you were in the hospital, and I just about lost it. Thank God you're okay."

Maddie blinked. "Uh, it's no big deal."

"But you almost got a concussion."

"Yeah…about that." Heat crawled up Maddie's neck. "I can't stand the sight of blood, which made me faint, and that's why I hit my head."

A few seconds ticked by as he seemed to take in that information. "Can't stand blood, huh?" His lips curved into a languid smile as he watched her. "Something new I learned about you."

She stared back at him. The tenderness in his gaze amazed her.

He looked up at her mom and sister, who were watching their interaction with avid interest. "She's damn lucky," he told them. "I just wish I could have been here sooner."

"You are so sweet," Louise said with a dreamy far-off look in her eyes.

Her mother nodded. "We all really appreciate you coming, Trent. Maybe we'll leave now, since you're here and can take her back to the house when she's discharged."

"Don't worry. I'll take good care of Maddie. In fact, I

don't plan on letting her leave my sight for the rest of the day."

Her mom walked over to him and gave him a peck on the cheek. "I know you will."

"We'll see you tonight at the rehearsal dinner," Louise said, opening the door for their mom. "Try and get some rest, Maddie."

"I'm on the case," Trent assured them. His attention traveled back to Maddie until his gaze locked on hers. "Even if I have to tie her to the bed myself."

Mercy. She swallowed as her abdomen tightened with longing.

Her mother and sister walked out but not before she caught the wink that Louise threw at her when Trent mentioned tying her to the bed. Leave it to her sister to not miss that comment.

"I need to get out of here," she told him once it was just the two of them.

She tried to get up but Trent pressed a hand on her shoulder, preventing her. "You'll leave when they say you can leave."

Maddie's temper flared. "Look, I'm starving and I'm sore. Now is not the time to get heavy-handed with me, buster."

"Somebody is cranky."

"Since when have hospitals become like airlines? I can't even get so much as a peanut here."

Trent made a *tsking* sound. "You're hysterical, too."

"I am not hysterical!"

His eyes sparkled and he leaned in, his gaze dipping to her mouth. "Then you might want to keep it down a bit.

We don't want your mom and Louise rushing back in here. Otherwise, they're going to see me do this," he murmured before his lips covered hers.

Oh, but that man knew how to mess with her already sore head. Especially when he left her mouth burning with fire. He pressed nearer, cupping her face in those steady hands of his. And she kissed him back. Kissed him with every ounce of energy she had left in her body after this exhausting morning. Her mind spun from the complete craziness of it all, while her body reveled in his touch. She was so glad he came to the hospital. That he stayed. That he didn't plan on leaving her side the entire day. It was an odd feeling for her to have—this security. This sense of being treasured. She hadn't felt like that since before her father left.

They finally broke apart, and his forehead came to rest on hers. "You know how to drive a man crazy. That's for sure."

"Uh, crazy in a good way, right?"

He kissed the tip of her nose. "Yes. Crazy in a good way."

"I bet this has been the most interesting job you've ever taken, huh?"

He cleared his throat as he moved away from her. "Yeah. You could say that."

"I'm sorry. My family hasn't made it easy for you. They're a bit pushy."

"I like your family."

She nodded, slightly disappointed he didn't add, *And I like you too*. "I need to get out of here. Michael's parents want the wedding party on their yacht this afternoon for a little cruise."

"I think you should take things slow because of your

injured hand. Everyone will understand if we're not there."

"Trent, I didn't lose a limb. I'm perfectly fine," she said, raising her stitched hand. "In fact, I never felt— Ow!"

Tears sprang in her eyes as she breathed through the pain of accidently bumping her hand on the bed rail.

"What was that about being fine?" His face dared her to argue.

"Okay, maybe I'm a little tender."

"See? Take it from someone who's played football injured and lived to regret it. Besides, Louise will have my head *and* yours if you aren't 100 percent by the wedding day."

"Yeah," she admitted with a crooked grin. "I guess you've got a point."

He bent his head and placed a kiss on her smiling mouth. "I never noticed how sexy you are when you admit I'm right."

"If you think I look good now, you should see me with a full stomach," she hinted.

"Well, as soon as you're discharged I'm going to treat you to the best hamburger drive-thru I can find on the way home."

"You're a complete god." Her voice was a sigh.

"I've been called that by women before."

And probably by more beautiful, less cursed women, too. "I'm sure you have."

Trent shifted on the bed, wrapping an arm around her shoulders. "Yeah, but I like how you say it best."

Maddie toyed with her fish platter as Michael and Louise posed for a few more pictures with the priest who would be conducting their ceremony. The restaurant they chose for the rehearsal dinner was a lovely mix of modern and old New England charm that boasted the best waterfront dining in town.

Her hand felt better and, after a hamburger and a quick nap, Maddie almost felt normal again. Or at least, as normal as a girl could feel with a gorgeous six-foot-two man watching over everything she did.

Trent's overprotective nature was extremely endearing, but she still couldn't quite figure him out. She kept waiting for him to wise up and realize that even without an injured hand, they just wouldn't work out together. He was Trent "Money" Montgomery, and she was "Fatty Maddie," who might have lost the weight but apparently not the curse.

Trent walked over and set a glass of ginger ale in front of her. Maddie had taken half a pain pill for her hand when she woke up so she could make it through the rehearsal dinner without any problems. As a result, Trent made sure she wasn't drinking any alcohol this evening. His thoughtfulness almost undid her.

"Are you feeling okay?" he asked, sitting down beside her.

No. I think I'm really starting to have feelings for you and as soon as I do, you'll be gone. It was the way things worked for her. Men always found something in her lacking.

She pasted on a smile. "I'm fine, why?"

He motioned to her plate with his chin. "You hardly touched your dinner."

"That's because you insisted on buying me the supersized

fries to go with my burger."

He took hold of a strand of her hair and rubbed it between his fingers. "Nothing's too good for my girl," he said with a grin.

His girl. That sounded nice, even if it wasn't entirely true. Her sister's wedding was the day after tomorrow and seemed to loom over her like the sword of Damocles. She was in no rush for the big day to happen because that meant her time with Trent could possibly come to an end.

Why on earth did she do this to herself? She *had* to fall for the one guy who was being paid to date her. She could just pummel herself.

She took a sip of her ginger ale then stared down into the glass, thinking that—and her spirits sank at the thought—maybe it was for the best that their relationship end quickly before she got further attached.

"You know Ryan has been giving me the death stare since we left the church," Trent commented, looking half amused and half pissed off.

"Really? What did you do to him?"

"I didn't do anything. Except stand in the way of him trying to play nursemaid to you."

"Oh, I doubt that. Ryan never struck me as the nurturing type."

"Well, jealousy does strange things to men. I guarantee you that if I wasn't here, he'd be all over you," he grumbled.

"Hmm…"

Trent narrowed his eyes. "That's all you have to say? *Hmm*?"

"I'm sorry. Should I have said something else?"

"Yes. Like how about…I'm glad you're here then. Or

better yet, how about…it doesn't matter that Ryan would be all over me because I would never take him back—oh, and he has hands like a girl."

She laughed. "You wanted me to say he has girl hands?"

"Yes. No." He shook his head. "But I mean, you have to admit, no normal man has hands that smooth."

"He did always wear gloves when he worked," she mused. "Oh, and speaking of work, Chef Dean emailed me a contact to call about a job. There's an opening at La Mer near Faneuil Hall in Boston."

He smiled. "That's fantastic, Maddie. I'm sure you'll get the job."

"Thanks. If I don't, Ryan told me during rehearsal that he would put in a good word for me at a restaurant in the Back Bay."

Trent's expression suddenly darkened. "Oh, did he now? You were going to accept help from a guy who caused you to lose your job in the first place?"

She shrugged. "I didn't take him seriously. I assumed it was his guilty conscience speaking."

"Guilty conscience my foot." A muscle ticked along his jaw. "He wants you back."

"Wait. I'm confused. Who is the jealous one here again?"

"Obviously, he is, since he can't take his eyes off you. In fact, you should probably kiss me now so he'll stop staring, and then I won't have to go over there and make him stop by punching him in both eyes."

He looked so disgruntled she almost laughed again, and because she found his petulant behavior so charming, she leaned over and brought her face close to his. "My hero," she said, her mouth moving closer until her lips pressed against his.

Her heart thumped wildly as he kissed her back. She loved the touch of him. Even a whiff of his cologne temporarily blanked out her mind. There was no doubt she was going to be in trouble come Sunday morning.

Someone behind them cleared her throat. Pulling back, she gazed up at her sister with a sheepish grin.

"Sorry to interrupt," Louise said with a roll of her eyes, "but Michael told me to tell Trent to go meet the rest of the guys outside on the deck. No women allowed apparently. Something about Scotch and cigars." She made a face.

Trent's mouth quirked up. "Well, if Michael insists…"

Louise smiled. "Unfortunately, he does."

He glanced at Maddie as if seeking her consent. "Are you okay?"

"I'm fine," she assured. She couldn't remember ever meeting a man so damn considerate. If only he'd perform one selfish act. Just one. Maybe it would squelch her growing feelings for him and give her heart a fighting chance. "My hand is fine. Go."

Trent leaned over and kissed her forehead. "Text me if you need anything."

Louise watched him go, her brow dipping into a deep *V*. She finally turned toward Maddie. "I'm sorry," she announced.

Confused, Maddie raised her brows and waited for her sister to say more.

"I'm sorry for feeling sorry for you. For thinking that I was the lucky one in our family."

She shook her head. "I don't understand, Louise."

"My career at Earthbound Publishing has been going great and then I meet Michael and quickly get engaged and…"

"My career is in the pits along with my love life?" she finished ruefully.

"I *used* to think that. But now, I envy you. So much so that I feel I'm making a mistake with Michael."

Panic turned Maddie's body cold. "Wh—what do you mean you're making a mistake?"

"I look at you and Trent and I'm thinking, I don't have that. But I want it. Why should I settle for anything less, right? I could be setting myself up for a divorce a few years down the line. You never lost hope, and look who you met up with again after all these years. Trent is your soul mate."

She gaped at her sister. *Oh, holy heaven, what have I done?* "You think Trent is my soul mate?"

"Of course he is. He's perfect. Everyone with two eyes can see that."

"Uh, he's not that perfect," she uttered lamely.

"Don't try and make me feel better. Trent is completely devoted to you. I love Michael, but he's never acted with me like Trent does with you. I'm so confused. I don't know how to break it off. What do you think I should tell Michael?"

Maddie leaned over and grabbed her sister's arm. "Nothing. You will say nothing and you will marry that man and live happily ever after. He loves you and you love him. You're just getting last minute wedding jitters."

Louise gazed at her, her eyes clouding with tears. "I don't think so."

Ohmygosh ohmygosh ohmygosh. Maddie was ruining everything. All because she was worried what other people would think of her. All because she hired a fake wedding date. She had to stop this train before it completely derailed her sister's future. "Please listen to me. You're making a mistake if you think that Trent and I have a perfect relationship."

"But I know what I see. And what I want."

"No. You don't, because it's all been a lie. And apparently a very good lie. *I'm* the one who should be sorry, Louise. Trent and I are not soul mates or in any kind of relationship. He's not even a real wedding date." She took a deep breath, but her words still drifted into a hushed whisper. "I hired Trent to come with me."

Chapter Ten

Maddie held her breath for what seemed like hours as Louise continued to stare at her. Unfortunately, when her sister finally did compose herself enough to open her mouth, nothing came out.

"I know it must seem completely idiotic to you," Maddie said, hoping to coax at least a grunt from her, "hiring a date to your only sister's wedding and all."

Louise slowly nodded.

"I mean, who does such things nowadays, right? Women don't need men for anything. Well, they do need them for *one* thing. But that's all—and, really, debatable depending on your sexual orientation."

Louise lowered her head and pressed two fingers to her eyes. Uh-oh. Her sister didn't look well. Complete hatred toward her or maybe a migraine was imminent.

Maddie licked her dry lips. "Louise, please, say something. You're making me nervous."

"Why would you feel the need to lie to me?"

The hurt in her sister's tone made her feel small and like the worst sibling on the planet. "I'm sorry, Louise. I—I didn't want you fussing and worrying about how I feel on *your* wedding day. You should be happy and enjoy your day. Then there was Veronica's smug comments that day at the dress fitting. Everything hit me then. I wasn't thinking that far ahead—or plain *thinking* at all—when I told you I was bringing someone to the wedding. I was just tired of coming off as the loser of the family all the time."

"You're not a loser, Maddie. I have never thought that." Louise looked down at her hand and began twisting her engagement ring. "Does Mom know you've been lying?"

Her shoulders sagged. "Of course not. And you can't tell her. At least…not yet. She's practically the president of the Trent Montgomery fan club."

"And I was about to become her vice president. He fooled us all." She heaved a sigh. "I'm really going to miss him after the wedding."

I'm going to miss him, too.

"How on earth did you end up hiring him?" she asked.

"He works for Match Made Easy. It was just a coincidence that we went to high school together. Dumb luck, really." *Dumb, dumb, dumb, cursed luck.*

"Gosh, I feel so stupid now. To think I almost called off my wedding because I thought my relationship wasn't as good as yours."

"Don't be. It's all my fault. Trent and I were better actors than we thought."

Louise gave her a long look, her eyes narrowing into two blue slits. "Was it really all an act?"

Maddie swallowed, debated on telling her sister how she felt about Trent and how he could be feeling for her. But in the end, she decided her confusion about their relationship might only hurt Louise and Michael's wedding. And that was the last thing she would ever want to do.

"I... Of course it was all an act," she lied. "That's what I'm trying to explain to you. What you saw between Trent and me wasn't real. So don't follow that. Follow your heart and what you feel for Michael."

"But I'm scared, Maddie. All this curse talk has me worried. I mean, I think about Mom a lot. Why would Dad leave like he did? He seemed happy with us. He loved us. He had to. Then all of a sudden he was out of our lives. Why would he do such a thing? I even tried to contact him. Sent him an invitation to the wedding and everything." She lowered her gaze to her lap. "He never responded."

Maddie banked down twenty-some-odd years of hurt herself and put up a brave front for her sister. "Screw him. It's his loss."

Louise gave her a reluctant smile. "Really?"

"Absolutely," she said with a confidence she didn't feel.

"Yeah, I guess it is his loss," Louise said, her smile broadening.

Maddie took hold of Louise's shoulders and met her gaze. "Now you be honest with me. Take out all the talk about the curse and Trent and everything else, and tell me how you feel about Michael."

Her sister didn't hesitate answering. "I love him," she said simply.

Thank God. "Good. I fully believe—and you have to, too—that there is no perfect relationship. Only a person who is perfect for you. And Michael is that person." Maddie had the same abandonment fears as Louise but felt her sister really had a shot at true happiness with Michael. At least Louise never seemed to have the man problems she had always endured.

Louise leaned in and gave Maddie a heartfelt hug. "You're right. I feel better about everything now. I guess I really was suffering from pre-wedding nerves." She paused, biting down on her lip. "So what happens now with you and Trent?"

Good question. "The charade must go on," she said with a shrug. "I still need to save face in front of Veronica and the rest of the family. Plus, Aunt Lois will be heartbroken if she finds out her duct tape bracelet is a flop."

"Duct tape bracelet?"

She held up her hand like a stop sign. "Long story."

Trent and Michael came back into the restaurant just then, smiling and laughing with each other. Sourness pooled in the pit of her stomach at the sight of them, like they were the best of friends.

More lies. Trent's actions weighed on her and made her chest grow tight. Or was their friendship real? She was deathly afraid to know for sure.

"Oh good, the guys are done and probably smelling of smoke," Louise said, wrinkling her nose. "It's a shame you and Trent aren't really dating. It looks as though they are hitting it off." She waved at her fiancé, and Michael blew her a kiss.

Maddie smiled at the sweetness of his gesture. Thank goodness Louise hadn't thrown away her future with Michael over something so meaningless as her temporary relationship with Trent.

Suddenly she felt, rather than saw, Trent's gaze on her. Out of curiosity, she glanced at him. Sure enough, when their eyes locked, she was hit with that same fluttering against her ribs she'd come to experience whenever she had his attention. So not good. Could a person fall for another in such a short time frame? It had to be the high of the wedding atmosphere that was making her go all tingly and hopeful.

Louise glanced back and forth between Trent and Maddie with a look her sister knew all too well; Louise's mind was definitely working overtime. "Are you sure Trent's devotion act is just part of what you hired him to do?" she whispered.

She wanted to say no. That Trent was no longer the player he'd been in high school and college and there was something more between them than just mere attraction and an escort service contract.

Against her better judgment, Maddie snuck another peek at Trent. Her breath caught in her throat when he gave her a smile that was steamier than a mug of hot chocolate. "Uh…" She swallowed hard. "Yes. He's very experienced at this sort of thing."

Louise fanned herself and muttered, "You can say that again."

Trent took hold of Maddie's uninjured hand and guided her down the few short wooden steps that led out to a deserted beach. He'd had enough of wedding chitchat, and of people in general, so before heading back to the house, he suggested a pit stop. After the ordeal at the hospital this afternoon and then the exhausting rehearsal dinner, he needed some downtime. Just him and Maddie. And now that they were alone, walking along the rocky sand with nothing around them but the lull of the waves and the moonlit sky, nothing felt more…perfect.

He hadn't thought he could ever feel this way. Wanting to put his heart on the line again. For so long he'd felt… unlovable. Even a failure. He could thank his parents and ex-fiancée for that. But Maddie was different. Her family was different. They liked him for who he was, not for who he'd been or what he could do. He was more himself around them. They welcomed him into their world as easily as breathing.

But then again, they thought he and Maddie were in a real relationship.

He had the chance to make things right, though. Maddie had become important to him. He realized it even more when he'd heard she was in the hospital. Hell, she was more than just important. He was falling for her. He felt it. Not to mention those sparks of attraction that went off whenever they'd touch in even the smallest ways.

She had to feel it, too. There was no denying that. But he'd wait until after the wedding to tell her the truth. Once they were back in the normal world away from the wedding hype and talk of curses, he'd explain everything about his cousin's business. How he was just helping Kennedy out and had no intention of trying to fool her or play games like the old Trent. Surely, she would understand that.

They continued to walk in silence. Despite her best effort to hide it, Trent caught Maddie's slight shiver. He removed his suit jacket and draped it across her shoulders, making her look as if she'd been wrapped up in a blanket instead.

"Better?" he asked.

She smiled. "Much. Thanks."

"It looked as though you and Louise had a nice long sisterly chat at dinner tonight."

They were mostly in shadows, but he still caught her smile dim a little. "Yes, I guess we did."

He hesitated. "Everything all good?"

"All good on the sister front."

"But not good on another front?" He hedged. Maddie seemed reserved tonight. Like they had gone in reverse or something. And he didn't like it.

"All other fronts are exactly as they've been." Then she turned and began walking again.

He followed, feeling a little off balance. It prompted him to open his mouth. "I like you," he blurted.

She stopped, didn't turn around.

"I really like you, Maddie." His voice was but a whisper in the darkness.

She finally looked at him, giving him a weak smile. "I like you, too. But I think we've established that already."

He shook his head. "No. You don't understand. Ever since Candace, I haven't really *liked* a woman in a long time—let alone allowed myself to have any stronger feelings than that. There was a long time in high school when I barely even liked myself. When I think back on those times, I'm glad I didn't know you then."

She gave a self-depreciating laugh. "Fatty Maddie was way out of your league anyway."

"Maddie, don't."

"Don't what?"

"Don't put yourself down like that. You have a way of flashing your inferiority complex like an FBI badge. I was a spoiled, rich athlete who sought approval from other rich, spoiled athletes. You had every right to hate me back then. If anything, *you* were the one who was out of *my* league. I just had to do some growing up to realize that."

"Trent, why are you telling me all this?"

Why am *I telling her this?* He wasn't sure. All he knew was that he wanted to be honest about *something* with her and that he didn't want this weekend to end. Maddie had been hurt in the past by men. He didn't need a degree in psychology to figure out she had trust issues. And she was also a woman who desperately wanted to be loved. Which was why he was so determined not to mess this up but, because he evidently was an idiot and way out of practice, he was fumbling it.

He shook his head at himself. "I want you to know that I'm having a good time. I didn't think it was possible, but this wedding preamble has been sort of fun. But more so because it's been with you."

"Yeah, I guess we both really lucked out with Match Made Easy."

"*Riiiight.*" He stretched the word out slowly. "No doubt that Match Made Easy is a great company." He let a long minute pass as he banked down his frustration.

He took hold of her hand again, stroking the inside of her delicate fingers. "Would you date me if you didn't need to hire me?"

She cocked her head, seeming to think it over. Not quite the reaction he hoped for. Beads of sweat began to congregate on his forehead despite the cool ocean breeze. Then she gazed at him, her beautiful mouth curving into a lazy smile. "That depends. Would you date me if I wasn't paying you to date me?"

He laughed. "I can see we both matured so much since high school. I've said it before and I'll say it again, you do know how to drive a man crazy." He grinned and was about to bring his lips down to hers, but before their mouths could connect, she pressed a firm palm against his chest.

"Confession," she said. "I only partially hated you in high school."

"Partially hated?"

"Yes, well, one part of me completely hated you, and the other part might have harbored a secret crush on you. There. The elephant is out of the closet."

"I think you mean the cat is out of the bag." He regarded her with a perplexed smile. "Did you really have a crush on me?"

"Oh, don't act like you had no idea every girl in our high school fantasized about you on a daily basis."

"Well, maybe I had a small clue." Trent reached out, unable to resist playing with a lock of her curls. "But I'm not interested in hearing about every girl in high school. I'm interested in hearing about this girl. So did you fantasize about me?"

She rolled her eyes. "I knew I shouldn't have opened my mouth, but since you were being honest, I thought you should know the truth."

"Does this mean you really like football, too?"

"I'm afraid not," she said with a grave face.

He chuckled. "Damn. I knew it was too good to be true. But that's okay. I said I would make you a fan. You're not the first I've converted."

"I suppose that's true." Something flickered in the back of her eyes, and there was a sudden strain in her voice. "You must meet many women in your line of work."

"At the gym?" he asked.

"No, working for Kennedy."

"Ah," he said, looking away. "And this has you concerned?"

"Well, maybe. Do you always 'romance' your jobs?"

"No." He heaved a frustrated sigh. "Maddie, I can honestly say I've never romanced anyone I've been hired to date. But if you're inferring that I should come clean to Kennedy, I had in fact planned to do just that."

"You did? Oh, that at least makes me feel somewhat better."

He smiled. "Somewhat?"

"Sorry. I guess I can't get past it. You seem so comfortable with women, and I'm not so good with relationships—er, with men."

"That's okay. You don't need to be good with other men. Just me. And so far, you're doing just fine."

"Yeah, you say that now. Talk to me in two months. *If* we're still talking by then."

"I heard all the stories from your family, but I still don't believe in this WD-40 Effect you think you may have."

He could tell that even with his joking and verbal assurance, she still seemed concerned. He wanted so badly to tell her the truth. That he wasn't an escort and he had no intention of going anywhere. But he couldn't. Hoping to show her, he reached for her, slipping his arm beneath her neck. Her mouth melded with his in a deep sliding kiss. She tasted sweet and just a bit spicy—exactly like her personality. This was what he'd been waiting for all night. Perhaps even all his life.

Trent broke away first, his breathing ragged. "Did you feel that just then?"

"Are you flirting with me?"

He chuckled. "No, I'm talking about that *kiss*. It was like Rapunzel when the prince broke the curse by kissing her."

"I'm pretty sure that was Snow White."

"Whatever. The point is they shared a special kiss, there was no more spell, and the prince finally got to make out with his princess."

She linked her hands around his neck. "That's a good way to end a fairy tale," she said with a sigh.

He nipped her bottom lip then grinned. "True. But in real life, it's an even better beginning." And he hoped once the truth was out, they'd still have their own.

Chapter Eleven

Maddie chewed on her cuticle as she watched the woman at the nail salon brush each coat of polish on her sister's toenails with the meticulousness of a Claude Monet wannabe.

Maddie couldn't take it anymore. She was a wreck. A complete wreck. Her sister was the one getting married tomorrow, and yet she was the one who couldn't form a single coherent thought. She had Trent Montgomery on the brain, and she needed to talk to somebody about it. Unfortunately, due to the bizarre nature of it affecting Louise's good spirits about the wedding, she didn't want to confide in her sister.

"You're awfully quiet," her sister commented, admiring the coral-color polish she'd chosen.

"Am I?" She switched fingers and continued chewing.

"Yes, is anything wrong?"

"Wrong? Nothing is wrong." Unless you counted the slight variable factor that after a little less than two weeks she could be falling for her hired wedding date.

Her best friend Sabrina and her husband, Jack, finally walked into the salon shop. Sabrina looked overheated and frazzled, while Jack on the other hand appeared as usual: about as polished and poised as a member of the royal family.

"Thank goodness we found you guys," her friend said with a heavy sigh. "Michael told me it was Diva Nails but he didn't bother mentioning there are three in town with the same name."

The receptionist shrugged. "We like to keep it all in the family, honey."

"Finally!" Maddie said, bolting from her chair.

"You can say that again," Jack muttered.

Maddie kissed Jack on the cheek, then gave her friend a tight hug. "I'm so glad you're here," she whispered in her ear.

Sabrina arched a brow. "I've missed you, too." She lowered her voice. "Or have you had enough of Veronica's company?"

"I had enough two weeks ago," she murmured, then whirled around.

"Sabrina is dying of thirst," she announced to her sister and cousins. She had to speak to Sabrina alone as soon as possible and needed to get her out of there. Maddie glanced over and implored her friend with her eyes to play along.

"Uh, yeah," Sabrina stated slowly. "I'm parched."

Jack glanced at his wife with alarm. "You can't get dehydrated. It's not good for—"

"Anyone!" Sabrina blurted. "Dehydration is not good for anyone. Especially on such a hot day."

Maddie frowned, thinking they both needed to dial down the acting. "Maybe we should go grab a drink down the street."

Veronica pointed to the back of the salon. "There are bottles of water back there."

"Plus, you just got here," Louise added.

Maddie elbowed her friend. "Uh, that's okay," Sabrina said, glancing at Maddie for confirmation. "I'm very particular about what I drink."

"I'll get you a bottle of Gatorade," Jack suggested. "There's a convenience store around the corner."

"No!" Maddie and Sabrina said at the same time, and Jack's brows climbed an inch up his forehead.

Maddie swallowed. "Um, I mean, Jack, you are so sweet but I don't want to hold you up. The guys are waiting for you back at the house."

"Okay." Jack spiked his fingers through his hair then looked at his wife again. "Brie, are you sure? Maybe I can get you one of those nasty kale drinks you like so much."

Sabrina snort-laughed. "Honey, I'm fine. Plus, this is a no-man-zone if you haven't noticed. Maddie and I will go get something to drink and come right back here. I promise."

"All right. But text me if you need anything."

"I will." She leaned up and kissed him soundly on the mouth. When she pulled back, Jack brushed his knuckles across her cheekbone with a simmering gaze.

Maddie held in a sigh at the obvious love between them.

Jack swung open the door and looked back at Sabrina again. "You have your cell phone, right?" Smothered chuckles came from the other bridesmaids.

"OMG, you need to leave now before you scare Louise into thinking all men turn psycho once they get married."

"Actually, I kind of already suspected that," Louise said

with a sheepish grin, creating more chuckles from the women.

Jack laughed, too. "Okay, okay. I'm out of here."

Maddie rolled her eyes toward the ceiling when he finally left. Sheesh. Did everything in her life have to be unbelievably complicated?

Maddie began pulling her friend out the door and realized too late that she'd smudged her toenail. Louise wasn't going to be happy. "We'll be back in a jiffy," she told the girls.

"Maddie, what on earth is wrong with you?" her friend asked as she was ushered down the street.

"I need someone to talk to, and I need a drink. We can accomplish both at that tavern down there."

"Okay, but just so you know, I can't drink with you."

Maddie stopped and gaped at her friend. "You're not."

"I am." Sabrina's grin radiated a thousand watts. "I'm due in January. Must have gotten pregnant on my honeymoon," she said with flushed cheeks.

She wrapped her arms around her friend and squeezed. "I'm so happy for you. Wow, I can't believe Jack is going to be a father. How's he taking it?"

Sabrina shook her head. "Not well."

"He doesn't want kids?"

"Oh, no, it's not that. He's thrilled about becoming a father. It's me being pregnant that he hasn't been dealing with well. He almost didn't let me drive here myself. Actually, I can't believe he even allowed me within a five mile radius of a nail salon. Didn't want Junior here," she said, affectionately patting her belly, "inhaling all the nail polish fumes."

Maddie laughed. "He's cute."

"He's annoying," she said with an affectionate grin.

"Well, you can watch me drink then." They walked into

the old English-style tavern and slid into a booth in the bar area.

Once Sabrina ordered a club soda and Maddie ordered her white wine, Sabrina folded her hands on the table and asked, "So, what's going on? Did you and Trent break up?"

Maddie turned her attention to her painted nails and cleared her throat. "Not exactly."

"What do you mean, not exactly? You're either going out or you're not."

She bit her lip, figuring out a way to ease into the truth. "Well, it's more like, we *weren't* going out. But now we plan to. After the wedding."

Sabrina sat back and stared. "I might need that drink."

Maddie sighed. "Look, no one else but Louise knows this, so you have to pinkie swear not to tell anyone. Promise?"

"I promise."

"Not even Jack."

Sabrina hesitated a moment then raised her hand, sticking out her pinkie finger. "Fine. Pinkie swear."

Their pinkies interlocked for a brief second, then Sabrina raised her eyebrows and waited.

Maddie sucked in a lungful of air then let it all out in one rushed breath. "I hired Trent to be my wedding date."

Sabrina blinked. "You *hired* a wedding date?"

She nodded weakly.

"Wow. I've never known anyone to do anything like that." Her voice dipped into a hushed tone. "What services are actually included in the price of one of those?"

"Sabrina! It's not like it's a prostitution ring." Not that those same little details didn't cross her mind when she first read the contract.

"Right. Sorry. But why did you do that? I could have asked Jack to set you up with another one of his friends if you were that desperate for a date."

"Because the last date you guys set me up on was a disaster, and I thought it would be better if I could call the shots and have him look completely smitten with me. And you know, if I let my family believe that I had been in a relationship for months, I could squash the, uh, curse rumors for a while, too."

Sabrina's eyes widened. "Oh, right. *The curse.* We should have asked Madame Butterfly about that the last time we went for a tarot card reading."

Maddie snorted. "That hack?"

"Madame Butterfly is *not* a hack. Misunderstood, yes. And perhaps confused about her gender, but not a hack."

"Whatever," Maddie muttered.

Madame Butterfly was a cross-dressing psychic she and Sabrina had gone to last year for love advice. And for laughs. Or at least, laughs to Maddie. Sabrina happened to be superstitious and took the advice that Madame gave her very seriously. Unfortunately, the psychic lucked out in her predictions, which only flamed Sabrina's belief in the woman-man's abilities.

"She told me that David and I would get back together, remember? And we did. Briefly. Also, she told me that she saw my future husband in a white coat. Jack had a white coat," Sabrina stated with a satisfied smirk.

Maddie just rolled her eyes.

"Okay, ye-of-such-little-psychic-belief, do you remember Madame Butterfly's prediction for you?"

"Actually, I do. She said she saw lots of hair in my future."

"Trent's not a hairy guy?"

"He's practically part seal."

Sabrina frowned. "Well, that's weird. Then maybe Trent isn't going to be part of your future."

Pain squeezed her heart as soon as she heard the words. She knew Sabrina didn't mean to be so blunt; to her, the reasoning seemed logical. But even though Maddie knew all that psychic stuff was nonsense, it still caused her to worry.

"I'm sorry," Sabrina said, placing a hand on Maddie's arm. "That didn't come out right."

Maddie shook her head. "Don't worry about it. You know I couldn't care less about what Madame Butterfly has to say."

"Of course. Look, don't listen to me. I must be suffering from preggo brains already," she said with a rueful smile. "So, you're pretty serious about Trent then, huh?

Maddie thought about that. "Yeah, I think I'm really falling for him. I've been feeling awful."

"What are your symptoms?"

"Can't concentrate, irritability, loss of appetite."

"Oh, boy. You've got it bad—or possibly lead poisoning."

Maddie would rather have the lead poisoning. At least there was a cure for that. But this… It was nauseating.

Sabrina's lips curved into a small smile. "Based on your silence, I'm going to say it's definitely *not* lead poisoning."

The waitress brought their drinks and a bowl of oyster crackers to the table. As Sabrina dug into the crackers like they were the only lifejacket on a sinking ship, Maddie's phone rang. She frowned when she saw it was from Kennedy Pepperdine.

A trickle of nerves crept up Maddie's spine. "Um, I think

I should take this," she said to Sabrina before answering the phone.

"Hi, Maddie?" asked Kennedy. "This is Kennedy Pepperdine from Match Made Easy."

"Hi, Kennedy, what can I do for you?"

"Well, I hate to tell you this since I know your sister's wedding day is tomorrow and all, but your check bounced."

"Oh, I'm sorry. It did?"

"Yes, but you did leave a credit card number in your file as a backup. I was wondering if you would like me to put the amount and the balance on that?"

Her cheeks felt about five hundred degrees. "Oh, uh, yes. That would be great."

"Wonderful. How is everything going with Trent anyway?"

Her eyes widened. "W-what do you mean?"

"Are you guys having a good time?"

"Yes, he's been...great."

"I'm so glad to hear that. I knew he would come through for you. He's very popular with the ladies."

"Is he? Well, Trent is very handsome," she admitted. "I suppose that makes him a sought-after request."

"That and Trent always makes sure his clients feel special. That's part of the service with Match Made Easy."

Part of his service.

Maddie fought the rising bile in her throat. "Um, did Trent happen to mention anything to you...about us?"

"No. Why? Did anything happen?"

"Um, no. I guess not." *Stop being so sensitive, Maddie.* Maybe Trent hadn't had a chance to mention her to Kennedy yet. Maybe he had every intention but his cell phone suddenly died or Kennedy had to take another call or...

There could been another reason. Trent may not want to go out on a real date with her after all. It could have been pretend.

Kennedy let out a light laugh on the other end of the line. "Whew, you had me worried there for a second. I'm glad to hear you've been pleased with our professionals. I'll go ahead and run the balance through your credit card and send you a receipt via your email. Sound good?"

Nothing was out of the ordinary. Everything was professional. Kennedy was doing her job—a job Maddie had hired her to do. Yet, it suddenly felt very out of the ordinary.

"Sounds good," she croaked. "Thank you, Kennedy."

"My pleasure. And if you ever need us again, don't hesitate to call."

"Right." Her vision blurred with unshed tears. Hopefully, she wouldn't ever need to use them again, but things didn't look promising. She ended the call and glanced up at Sabrina.

Sabrina took one look at her and stopped chewing. "What's the matter?'

She shook her head, afraid to speak or else she might burst into tears.

"Maddie, what has you so upset? Who was that on the phone?"

"The owner of Match Made Easy. My check bounced." Her lips trembled.

"Oh, please, don't cry. If you need the money—"

"No, that's not the problem. Although that is depressing in itself. What's so awful is that Trent didn't tell his boss about us."

"Did he say he would?"

She nodded. "Trent assured me he had every intention

of telling her. Just not when. But I had kind of hoped he'd say something before the wedding."

"He could still tell her the truth before tomorrow," she offered.

Maddie squeezed her eyes in pain. "To think, I was starting to believe his act. He really made me feel…special."

"You are special."

She raised an eyebrow. "Specially cursed, you mean?"

Sabrina smiled. "No. But in all seriousness, maybe you are becoming more than a job to him."

Maddie buried her face in her hands. "I don't know," she moaned. "Sometimes I feel that way and then other times I just think he sees me as he did in high school. And then I think why would someone like Trent want someone like me?"

"What do you mean by someone like Trent?"

"You know, football-Adonis-extraordinaire playboy who has more women throwing themselves at him than Tom Brady."

"Sounds like *you* still see Trent as he was in high school."

She lifted her head. "You think that's what I'm doing?"

"I do. Give Trent a chance. It's about time you gave any man the opportunity."

Maddie's heart lifted a fraction. "Maybe you're right."

"Of course I am. I'm smarter than the average friend," she said with a grin. "But sometimes it takes an outside perspective to see things the clearest. You were able to give me good feedback about all my problems with Jack. And everything turned out great in the end." She paused and smiled. "Eventually."

"I'll try to keep the eventually part in mind."

Sabrina laughed. "Good. So, let's see," she said, cocking her head in thought, "if I have the story straight. You hired Trent as your wedding date, but he eventually turned out to be a real date?"

"Pretty much."

"That's certainly a story for the grandkids."

Maddie raised her wine in salute. "From your mouth to Trent's ears."

"Yes, but let's not tempt fate," Sabrina said, crossing her fingers, "and hope he has hairy ears. After all, there just has to be something more between you two."

Maddie stopped mid sip. "There has to be?"

"Of course. No one is *that* good of an actor."

Right. And she could tell acting. Trent was attentive and affectionate. He laughed with her and made her laugh. Besides, no one could charm her and her family so well without at least a little bit of truth behind those actions. Unless…of course…

It happened to be his job.

Trent knocked on the bathroom door for the third time. "Maddie, Louise called. *Again.* She said the hairdresser is at the main house waiting for you. If you don't get over there soon, I can't be held responsible for any course of action your sister may take."

After a few beats, the door swung wide, and Maddie appeared. He opened his mouth but all he could think was *mine* and how she was the most beautiful woman he'd ever seen. She wore a strapless dark gray gown that accentuated creamy white shoulders that made a man itch to trace the curves. As she teetered in the doorway on three-inch heels, he didn't think she could have ever taken his breath away more than she already did. But he stood corrected.

He knew she was waiting for him to say something. But there were no words good enough. "You're lovely."

She smiled shyly. "Just wait until I get my hair and makeup done."

"You look perfect as you are," he said, wrapping her in his arms.

Maddie slid her arms around his neck, then tilted her head to the left.

"What are you doing," he asked, pulling back. "Were you checking out my ears?"

She quickly straightened, looking guilty and completely adorable. "Huh? No." She gave a weak cough. "Why would I ever do that?"

His lips twitched. "I'm afraid to find out."

"Well, you can relax. You're perfect. And hairless," she muttered.

"Is that bad?"

Before she could answer, there was a pounding at the door. "Maddie, if you don't come out of this room in two seconds, I will kick open the door and drag you out by your pearl earrings myself."

Maddie gave a weak smile. "It's the wedding. Louise isn't herself."

"You think?" He turned, wasting no time in answering the door.

Louise's hands were fisted on her hips and, although she was in running shorts and an old T-shirt, her hair was dramatically swept up high on her head with little white flowers around her ears traveling all along the back of her head like a debutante.

"Oh, hello, Trent," she said coolly. "I didn't realize you were still here. You should be grabbing brunch on the patio."

"I would have but I wanted to stick around in case Maddie needed help getting dressed."

Louise dropped her arms and marched in. "Well, that's very kind but your services are no longer required. I can take care of my sister's needs now."

Trent raised his brows. *My services are no longer required?* What had gotten into her? Under normal circumstances, they would be cracking jokes with each other already. Louise definitely had a prickly stick up her butt this morning, but he decided to let it pass, since he assumed it was a wedding-day-Bridezilla thing she had going on.

Trent glanced at Maddie, who seemed stiff as well. *Everybody* was acting weird. He knew there was more than one reason he didn't like weddings.

"Seeing that I'm no longer needed…" *Or wanted. Or barely tolerated.* "I'll go grab something to eat. Do you want me to bring you anything, Maddie?"

"I—"

"My mom has some snacks waiting for her already. You can go," Louise said, giving him an impatient wave.

Trent blew out a breath. "I guess I'll see you both at the church then." He wanted to kiss Maddie good-bye, but Louise planted herself in front of her sister like an impenetrable wall. "Good luck, Louise."

"Thanks."

Trent's gaze wandered one more time to Maddie, who

only shrugged at Louise's attitude, then he closed the door behind him and left.

Maddie turned to her sister. "That was rude."

"Sorry. It's stress. But it's not like you guys are a real couple."

Maddie looked at her nails, unable to meet Louise's gaze. She hated keeping things from her sister. She already told Sabrina. She might as well just tell Louise, too, now that things were in fact becoming real with her and Trent, since it was highly unlikely that information would affect the wedding. "Um, actually, Louise—"

"Plus, I'm kind of mad at him."

Maddie closed her mouth and blinked. "You're mad at Michael?"

"No, *Trent.*"

"Why are you mad at Trent?"

Louise walked over to the mirror and began fussing with her already perfect hair. "Last night I found one of his stupid business cards for Match Made Easy in Michael's sport coat."

"So? Maybe he just wanted to give Michael his contact number."

Louise looked at her. "Normally I would have thought that, too, but I asked Michael about it, and he said Trent gave it to him because he wanted to drum up some advertising venues for Match Made Easy. If that's the case, Trent has definitely been working overtime. Maybe he gets a commission out of it."

Maddie suddenly felt ill and sat down on the bed.

"I suppose it's his job," Louise went on, "but could you please tell him to tone it down at the reception? I don't want him thinking he can work the room like a used car salesman. What if people put two and two together and figure out you used Match Made Easy? Although it looks as if Veronica might need those services soon, too. I think she and her boyfriend are on the outs. All she did was complain about him this morning as she was getting her hair done." She checked her watch. "And speaking of hair done, we need to get yours done now."

Maddie sat frozen, afraid to move or else she'd throw up. Trent sure found time to promote his services. He was still a player. A very convincing player. She was obviously just a job to him. Nothing more.

Why had she expected anything different?

Louise laid a hand on her shoulder and gently squeezed. "Hey, it's not that big a deal. Put it behind you, use Trent for everything you paid him for, and have a great time tonight at the reception." When Maddie remained silent, Louise happily added, "And look on the bright side, come tomorrow, you'll never have to see him again."

Never see him again. The story of her life. She'd gone through this scenario of never being good enough for a man to love so many times she could write the playbook. But this time it was different. This time her heart was china, thrown to the ground and shattered by the hands of a man she thought was different.

Never see him again.

Maddie glanced up at her sister's reassuring face and solemnly nodded.

Chapter Twelve

Maddie had summoned an inner Herculean strength to get through the morning without falling apart. But she was determined for Louise's wedding day to be perfect. Even if her insides felt as crumbly as a cookie.

She stood behind her sister at the altar. Louise and Michael held hands, grinning and staring into each other's eyes like they were the only ones in the world. Maddie held in a sigh. *This is what true love looks like*, she thought. True happiness for all the world to see. Not secret agendas and misery weighing her down like a steel barbell.

She gazed out into the church and found Trent sitting just a few rows back. Sun streamed in through the stained glass, highlighting the reddish tones in his dark hair. He was—in a word—gorgeous with those firm features and confident set of his shoulders. He flashed his muscle-melting smile, and her cynical self couldn't help but believe it was just part of his job.

Closing her eyes, she cursed her own stupidity for ever thinking Trent could be different. He was just as self-centered as he'd been in high school.

"You may now kiss the bride," the priest announced.

As Louise and Michael kissed, the crowd clapped with approval. The organ music began, and the wedding party made their descent down the aisle. The photographer's camera snapped away, and as Maddie felt Trent's steady gaze on her, she struggled to keep her smile pleasant and in place.

Once the church had emptied out and the last group shot had been taken, Maddie finally found the courage to approach Trent waiting for her.

"You're dazzling," he said, offering her his arm.

The natural pull to go to him was strong. She wanted so badly to take his arm and lean in, but she kept her hands at her side. "Thank you. But you should probably save that kind of talk for when people are around."

He dropped his arm and studied her a moment. "I didn't say it for other people to hear. I said it because it's the truth."

"Is it? Because if so, I believe it's the first time you've told me the truth since I hired you."

He went speechless as a dawning look of realization hit his face. "I didn't want you to find out this way. I was going to tell you that Kennedy was my cousin after the wedding," he explained.

Her laugh was strained. "Funny enough, *that* I didn't know. But it does explain a few things. And at least I can say you're being honest with me now."

"Maddie," he said, reaching for her.

She slapped his hand away. "Don't Maddie me. Louise told me you gave your business card to Michael. You've been busy. Well, I can tell you, we both don't appreciate you trying to drum up more business for yourself, especially on my time."

"It's not like that, Maddie. Nobody knows I work for them. I was just trying to get some advertising for Match Made Easy. That's all and— Wait. Louise knows you hired me?"

She nodded. "I told her yesterday. Sabrina knows, too."

His brows lifted. "Why did you tell anyone? You said you didn't want Louise worrying about you. I thought the whole point was for people to stop thinking you're cursed and to have them stop feeling sorry for you."

"That was before. Now I want the game to end. In case you need it spelled out, you're fired."

He threw up his hands in frustration. "Well, that's just great. You're firing me. I don't even really work for Match Made Easy. I was just doing my cousin a favor."

Oh, lordy. She leaned on the end of a pew. Her instincts were dead-on about him. What other "truths" had he neglected to tell her?

"Look, you don't understand. Kennedy needed me. She was hoping that if I could pose as your wedding date and try to work in some advertising spots with Michael, it would really help her business. So I agreed to do it. But I wasn't trying to use you, Maddie."

She wiped at her tears, furious with herself for allowing them to form, let alone fall. "Right. And I should believe you now *because…*?"

"Because if you stop and really listen to what I'm saying, you'll know it's true. I loved spending this week with you. And not because I was hired to do it."

Her heat shifted rhythm. The words were what she wanted to hear, but she couldn't find it in herself to believe them. "This isn't working for me anymore. I think it's best if we end this agreement now. I can make up some excuse as to why you're not at the reception."

"Maddie, you're doing it again." His tone was low and urgent.

"What am I doing?"

"Pushing men away. Pushing *me* away."

"That's ridiculous. Don't try and go Dr. Phil on me. You were hired for a job and that's it. The wedding is over, and the job is done. There's nothing between us to push away." She hiked up her dress and whirled around, her breaths coming out in short heavy pants. She made it halfway down the aisle before Trent grabbed her wrist, stopping her.

"You know, when I first heard all the stories about your men issues and how the family thought you were cursed, I actually felt sorry for you," he told her.

She snorted. He felt sorry for her. *Join the club.*

"But I now know you created those problems yourself."

Her chin shot up, and she glowered at him. "I have no idea what you're talking about."

"Don't you? You create your own problems and concerns because you're afraid. Afraid you'll become attached to someone. So you don't ever try. Because you know as soon as that happens, you'll have to trust him. So you fall back on the tired excuse of this curse and push men away before they can leave you. That way you'll never get hurt."

She gasped. "That's a horrible thing to say."

"Only a man who wants to get closer to you and cares would dare to say it. Don't throw away what we could have because it's easier and safer. Take a chance for once. I'm willing to take a chance on you." Imploring her with his gray-green eyes, he held out his hand. And waited.

She studied it, trying to gain the courage and believe his words. She wanted to. She was tempted to trust, but in the end old fears wrapped around her like a straightjacket, and she kept her arms at her sides.

He heaved a frustrated sigh. "So that's it then?"

"I'm sorry," she whispered.

For a long moment their eyes met. Then he leaned in and kissed her on her cheek, his lips lingering painfully longer than she could bear before he pulled back. "I'm sorry, too."

*B*ottoms up.

Maddie tossed down another tequila shot then wiped her mouth with the back of her hand. The bartender winced when she slammed the glass a little too hard on the bar.

"You're flagged," he told her with a explicit look.

"Party pooper." She only had two shots, but she'd always been a bit of a lightweight. She swiveled around on the stool.

Her blurred gaze traveled over the crowd of guests at the reception. Michael and Louise were in each other's arms slow dancing to their wedding song, "Our Love is Here to Stay." One of the singers then announced for the rest of the wedding party to join them in their dance.

Great. The worst part of the maid of honor's duty.

Before she could even stand, Ryan was at her side. "I believe that means maid of honor and best man share a dance," he said with a glint in his eyes.

She shrugged. "Sure. Let's do this," she said. The tequila was finally having the effect she wanted, and walking became a bit of an effort. Ryan seemed unfazed by her condition and simply held her arm as he led her to the dance floor.

She linked her hands behind Ryan's neck and swayed with him to the music. She hoped he wouldn't get chatty all of a sudden. The lyrics of the song were pretty, and she wanted to listen to them. Her head was nice and fuzzy, and she was even starting to forget all about Trent.

"So where's your boyfriend?" Ryan asked.

Almost starting to forget about Trent.

"Gone," she murmured, hoping there'd be no follow-up questions.

"Ah. Another one bites the dust?" Amusement edged his tone.

Her gaze cut to him, sharp and direct. "What does *that* mean?"

"Nothing. I didn't think that guy would last. Although I thought he would stay at least until dinner was served," he said with a wry smile.

"Yes, well, we had different views on what we both expect out of relationships." Like honesty and commitment. "It was for the best that I end it before there were any real hurt feelings."

"I have to give him points for lasting as long as he did. You were always kind of hard to get close to."

She tripped on his foot, fell into his chest, then righted herself. "What did you say?"

Before he could answer, the song ended, and the band began to play a more upbeat tune. More people started funneling in around them.

"Let's go grab a drink," he suggested.

"The bartender won't serve me," she shouted over the music. "And you didn't answer my question. Are you saying I'm difficult to be with?"

He shook his head. "Not at all, Maddie. I'm sorry I said anything." Then he gave her one last pitying look and walked away.

Good riddance. She didn't want to hear Ryan's opinion anyway. What did he know? Maddie made her way through the crowd and back to the bar. She didn't want to feel anymore, just wanted to blend in and forget. She flopped down on a stool and hoped she could get a drink. But the bartender saw it was her and immediately placed a club soda in front of her.

Everyone was against her tonight.

She made a face. "Thank you."

"You will be thanking me," he said with a smirk before waiting on a couple at the other end.

"Doubt that," she muttered, scowling at the fizzing glass.

"What do you doubt, dear?" her mother said, sitting down next to her.

Everything. But mostly myself. "I doubt I'll ever be as lucky as Louise," she answered instead.

Her gaze wandered to her sister. Louise and Michael were talking to Aunt Marie. They were both nodding and laughing, enjoying the celebration. Just the way Maddie had hoped the night would turn out for her sister.

Her mom wrapped an arm around her shoulder. "I haven't seen Trent since the ceremony," she said gently. "Is he feeling okay?"

Maddie swallowed. This was her chance to continue the lie. To save face. Her mother had practically dropped the excuse right in her lap. She could tell everyone that Trent had become ill and had to go back to the house. Easy peasy and no one would be the wiser.

"Yes, Trent wasn't feeling..." She gulped hard. "His complexion was really..." She could feel her throat closing up. She looked up at her mom as a hot tear slipped down her cheek.

"Oh, honey, what is it?"

"Mom, I got scared. And now Trent's gone. Just like Dad."

Her mom ran a hand down her arm. "Honey, you can't compare the two."

"Then why isn't Dad here on Louise's big day? She told me she invited him to the wedding. Does he really want so little to do with us? I don't understand what we did to drive him away."

"You didn't do anything."

"Then why did he leave us? The curse?"

Her mom *pfffd*, flopping her wrist in the air. "He didn't leave because of any curse. He left because I told him to leave."

"What?"

"I'm sorry. I suppose you girls were old enough to hear the truth years ago, but I wanted to give your father a chance to become sober."

Maddie took a steadying breath. Almost couldn't say the words. "Dad is an alcoholic?"

"I'm afraid so. When you girls were little, he was more of a binge drinker. I thought he had some sort of control over it. But then it got away from him, and he started drinking even on the days he had to work. *When* he made it to work."

"Oh, gosh, I never noticed anything out of the ordinary."

"You weren't supposed to. I was careful to shield those things from you and Louise. Made sure you had playdates away from the house when he had a particularly bad bout. Even made sure he stayed overnight in a motel if he'd been drinking and needed to dry out. Needless to say, it was exhausting and getting harder and harder to hide, so I finally had to give him an ultimatum. Us or the alcohol."

"And he didn't choose us," she said softly.

Her mom shook her head. "I was afraid he'd lose his job if they found out, so I just let people think he left us for other reasons. He wanted to be here today, though. Although he's been in and out of rehab, he still can't seem to stay sober for too long after. I know he's embarrassed."

"Oh, Mom. All this time. I thought maybe it had been me. That stupid curse."

"Never, honey. It was him. But don't doubt that he loved you. Love *all* of us."

The truth settled in, and she let it churn in her mind. It looked like Trent had a point, after all. Had she lived her life hiding behind the excuse of that curse? She threw it in Trent's face enough times. Well, maybe it was time for her to stop hiding.

From everyone.

"Mom, I have a confession to make."

"What is it?"

A loud amplified whistle cut through the air. "Ladies and gentlemen, may I please have your attention?" Maddie looked at the far end of the room and saw one of the band members beckoning her to come to the stage. Ryan was there waiting with a note card in his hand ready to give his best-man speech.

Maddie hugged her mom. "Never mind. It'll come out soon enough."

The band leader smiled at her as she approached. "Let's give it up for the maid of honor, Maddie McCarthy, folks!" Applause and hoots erupted from the crowd.

Maddie cleared her throat and took the microphone. "Good evening, everyone. I had something prepared but sometimes you have to go with the moment, so humor me. For those of you who don't know me, I'm Louise's older sister. And for those of you who *do* know me, you're probably wondering how I ever got this job." Laughter punctuated the comment, which she nodded to recognize. "Yes, I'm hardly the love expert in the family, but that doesn't mean a person has to give up hope of finding that special someone. Someone you take a leap of faith with and trust with all your heart. My sister didn't give up, and I'm thrilled she found a man who complements her so perfectly. My relationship with Louise is very special to me, so I would never give her up to anyone who I didn't think was worthy of her love and worthy of her trust. I look forward to the future for these two. Louise and Michael seem to have that certain something about them. I didn't fully understand until I experienced a taste of that feeling myself. But now I know that theirs truly will be a match made in heaven. So ladies and gentlemen, can I ask that you join me in toasting the bride and groom by raising your glasses. To Michael and Louise, all the happiness in the world."

Everyone in the room raised their glass then drank. She handed the microphone to Ryan and stepped off the stage.

Glancing at Trent's empty seat at the table, she felt her stomach sink. She had wanted Trent out of her life, but now she wondered if she truly had made the right decision to push him away.

"Where are you going, hunk?"

Trent lowered his suitcase to the ground and rubbed his hand over his jaw. "The name is *Trent*, Marie."

Maddie's aunt Marie grinned up at him. "I know." She glanced at his suitcase and frowned. "You're picking a funny time to leave. You haven't even danced with your Maddie yet."

His Maddie. Yeah, that was hardly the case.

After Maddie gave him the boot at the church, his only option was to go back to the house, pack, and quietly leave. He hadn't planned on running into family. He figured everyone would be at the reception by now.

"What are you doing here?" he asked.

She held up a prescription vial and shook it like a maraca. "Can't forget the old heart pills. Which I obviously did. The limo driver was kind enough to take me to the house. He's waiting now, so you can ride back with me."

Trent shook his head. "I'm not going to the reception."

Marie grabbed her heart, which automatically had him pulling out his cell phone in case he needed to dial 911. "Why on earth not? Maddie needs you."

"Needs me for what? I'm sure the best man will dance with her."

Marie harrumphed. "That girl doesn't need a temporary

dance partner. She needs a partner for life. And he is not it."

"I'm not it, either."

"You don't love Maddie?" She huffed out another breath. "Could have fooled me."

"I—" He wanted to refute Marie's statement. But he honestly didn't know what he felt for Maddie—besides that he missed her already and felt sick every time he remembered that she wasn't going to be a part of his life anymore.

"That's what I thought," she stated matter-of-factly.

He wearily sat down on his luggage. "You don't understand. She doesn't want to see me. We fought, and she told me to leave. And don't tell me it's because of that stupid curse, because I know for a fact it isn't."

Marie patted his back. "I know there isn't a curse."

He looked up through narrowed eyes. "You do?"

"Oh yes. I just humored the poor girl. She wanted something to blame for her bad decision-making so I let her do just that."

"Good grief," he moaned. He wished Maddie's family had told that information to Maddie months ago. "Well, there's nothing I can do about our relationship, anyway. She won't listen."

Marie flicked her wrist with a little shrug, sending the army of bracelets on her arm clanking. "My dear boy, there are more ways to apologize to a woman than by mere words alone."

He thought it over a minute then stood. Taking Marie's fragile hand into his own, he kissed the back of it. "You are a very wise woman," he told her.

Marie blushed. "Yes, I know. And I do hope that is one thing that *does* run in the family."

"Yeah." He smiled and sent her a slow wink. "Me, too."

Chapter Thirteen

Maddie rolled over in bed, wishing she had the fore-thought to pack pain reliever with her. Between the two tequila drinks and the on-again-off-again crying bout she had last night, her head felt like it was wrapped in a tourniquet.

I should only be so lucky.

A banging at the door had her burrowing under the covers. "Go away," she moaned.

"Maddie, open up," Sabrina said through the door. "Your mom wanted me to check on you, and I can't give her a full report until I see you with my own two eyes."

Maddie raised her aching head and threw back the covers. "All right, hold on." She shuffled over to the door, a hand pressed up against her forehead, feeling as if that would prevent her brain from oozing out.

When Maddie swung open the door, Sabrina made a face. "You look like what I threw up for breakfast."

"Do me a favor and don't mention that when you report to my mom."

Sabrina closed the door behind her. "I brought you some aspirin to make you feel better." She held out her palm and a glass of water in the other hand.

Maddie took the pills for her headache. However, with Trent gone and her life in disarray, she doubted she would ever truly feel better.

"Honey, I know what you're going through. I didn't think I could feel any lonelier than the time I spent when I pushed Jack away."

Maddie shook her head and sat down.

"I'm sorry, Maddie."

"Not half as sorry as I am." She flopped backward on the bed. "I was obviously right about him, which makes me feel so much worse."

"What do you mean?"

She sighed. "Trent wasted no time in leaving once I told him I didn't need him at the wedding any longer and that I considered his contract fulfilled, so I really was just a job he was doing for his cousin."

"Hmm…then why did he leave you a check?" she asked.

Her head popped up. "What check?"

Sabrina slid the paper out from under her hairbrush on the bureau and held it up. "This check."

"Let me see." She grabbed it from her hand and stared at the amount. Trent had written it out for the entire three thousand dollars she had paid Match Made Easy. *Why would he do that?*

She looked at Sabrina. "I can't believe he paid for himself," she whispered.

Her friend arched an eyebrow. "I can't believe you paid three thousand dollars. I should look into that profession."

"Yeah, and your husband would kill us both." She glanced at the check again and saw a sticky note attached.

Left a message at Michael's office. Told him Fenway Park advertising off.

Trent

As she stared at his words, her heart began to hammer. Oh my gosh. This really proved what Trent had been trying to tell her. That she wasn't just a job to him. He took back the advertising—everything—to show her he was telling her the truth. The paper check she held between her fingers felt heavy and cumbersome as she recalled how he'd told her he needed money to pay off the loans to his gym. He sacrificed everything—including his own business. She felt even more foolish for firing him. Because he asked her to take a chance on him, trust him, and she turned her back.

What had she done?

"I have to find him," she murmured, her mind racing. "I can start with his gym."

"Or you can start with his address," Sabrina said, pointing to the check.

"Ah. Even better." She tossed the check on the bureau and raced toward the bathroom. "I'm jumping in the shower now. Tell Jack to pack up the car and be ready in thirty minutes. I don't have a car so you guys will have to drive me."

"Wow, you ready in less than an hour?" Sabrina folded her arms with a smirk. "It *must* be love."

Maddie stopped at the bathroom door and grinned. "I don't know if it's love. But for the first time in my life, I'm willing to take a chance and find out."

"What do you want me to tell your mom?"

Maddie cringed. Her mom. Her family. They needed to know the truth, too. If she were really to stop hiding from this so-called curse and face Trent, she needed to face them first. Or else her words to him would be meaningless.

Maddie squared her shoulders as her resolve pushed through to the surface. "Tell my mom I'll be down for brunch as soon as I get dressed."

Maddie grabbed a glass of orange juice and tossed it back like it was the tequila from last night.

"Um, good morning, sweetie," her mom said, kissing her cheek. "Sleep well?"

She picked up another glass of juice and gave her mom a look. "What do you think?"

"That you could use one of these," she said, holding out a plate of doughnuts.

Her mouth watered, but now was not the time to indulge her sorrows in sugar and fat—no matter how much she was tempted. She needed to get some things off her chest first. "No thanks, Mom. I'm not hungry."

"Is it because it's bothering you that people are asking where Trent is?"

Maddie glanced around the room filled with family and the wedding party minus the bride and groom. Everybody was so busy enjoying the brunch and hospitality of Michael's parents that no one noticed that she was even here. "No, but I suppose I should offer an explanation to them, anyway. The truth."

Her mom frowned. "What truth?"

"You'll soon find out."

"Are you sure you want to do that, dear?"

She pressed a hand to her stomach, waiting for the knots to untie. "Yeah, I'm sure. It's about time."

She walked over to the microphone stand that was left from the engagement party and flipped it on. "Hello? Testing one-two-three." Her booming voice settled the room quickly.

When she had everyone's attention, she raised her hand in a weak wave. "Uh, hi. I just wanted to thank Mr. and Mrs. Lyons for being such wonderful hosts. Even though they're Louise's in-laws, they feel like family to me, too, and I hope to find someone as wonderful as Michael someday as well. I haven't yet. But that's okay. Or actually, I might have met someone but I pushed him away before I could really find out."

Everyone just stared at her. Oh Lord, she was babbling. She licked her lips and decided to keep going while she still had the courage. "For years, people have thought there was a WD-40 curse in our family. That we had a knack for displacing men out of our lives. I was even starting to believe it myself. So to prove you all wrong, I hired a wedding date to come here with me."

"I knew it!" Veronica yelled from the back of the room. Out of the corner of Maddie's eye, she saw Aunt Lois elbow her in the ribs.

Maddie smothered a grin. "Well, I want to set the record straight once and for all, because I realized some things yesterday at the wedding. One, I'm never going to drink tequila again. And two, there actually is a curse. But it's not the WD-40 Effect and it doesn't apply to any other woman in the family. That's because I've been my own curse. I've been the one who's been wrongly affecting my own love life. But not anymore."

Dead silence filled the air.

Okay, not as popular as the maid of honor speech, she mused. But at least she got what she wanted to say off her chest and acknowledged that she was the one who caused her relationships to fail. She was the one who was in control of her own life.

As sucky as it was.

She was about to turn off the mic, then added, "Thanks for listening."

She gazed over at Jack and Sabrina and nodded to them to let them know she was ready to leave. Her insides felt ten times lighter with the truth out on the table. No one could pity her anymore now that she and everyone else knew she was the one in control. The next step was to find Trent to tell him that, too.

And officially break her own curse.

"I'm really sorry, Trent. I think I only made things worse for you with Maddie by what I told her."

Trent turned off the faucet where he was planning to give his dog a bath and shook his head. "It's okay. I doubt what you said really mattered that much, anyway."

When Kennedy had relayed to him the conversation she had with Maddie the day her check bounced, he'd just about fallen to his knees. But Kennedy hadn't known things were getting personal with Maddie. She was just trying to make Match Made Easy look better by pretending Trent was so good at his escort job. Not that what Kennedy had said about him carried much weight. He still felt Maddie was looking for any opportunity to push him away before she grew too attached. Blaming the curse was just an easy out.

Kennedy wrung her hands. "Maybe I should talk to her."

"No, but thanks," he said, raking a hand through his hair. "I'll try and call her once she's home from the wedding. By the way, I'm sorry if I blew your advertising gig with Michael."

She shrugged. "I was kind of acting like a psycho-bully chief executive anyway, but only because I knew you needed your money back. I'm sorry I put you in the position that I did. I want my business to succeed, but not if it messes up your life."

"I think I do a pretty good job of messing things up for myself. Now I don't have my money or my woman. Maybe I'm fooling myself into thinking that Maddie even wanted me. Now that she doesn't need me for a wedding date, I've become obsolete just like I became with Candace."

"Don't be silly, Trent. Maddie doesn't seem to be the kind of woman your fiancée was."

"I guess I was really hoping that I found a woman who wanted me for nothing else but…just me. Stupid, huh?"

Kennedy walked up to him and cupped his cheeks in her hands. "You are kind, handsome, thoughtful, good to your cousin and dog, and intelligent, to name a few of your best qualities. She must be nuts. And if she can't see what a great guy you are, then she doesn't deserve you."

His cousin's outrage almost made him smile. She was

better than any team of cheerleaders on the football field. "Thanks."

He had been tempted to call Maddie this morning, if only to hear her voice, to see how the reception had gone. Not that she would have talked to him. She'd made it pretty clear that she never wanted to see him again. He'd hoped his gesture would have spurred a response from her. Now he didn't know what to think.

So things would have to go on as usual for him. He'd concentrate on his business and his life just as he had. Without Maddie.

And miserably.

With a resigned sigh, he went in search of his dog. Like most dogs, Bella hated baths. Fortunately for him, there weren't many areas in his house where an Old English Sheepdog could hide.

Kennedy followed him down the hall and into the kitchen. "I guess now is not the time to tell you that I've met someone."

He stopped and whirled around. "Seriously?"

She smiled. "Seriously. It was kind of an experiment, really. I created my own technology that I'm going to start using at Match Made Easy. That's how I met Justin. Turns out we're totally compatible—just like the software said we'd be. We've been dating for more than three months now."

Trent rubbed his chin. "Brought together by microchips and wires. How romantic."

"You just don't understand romance, my dear cousin. Besides, can you imagine what kind of publicity it could warrant if things *do* become serious between us?"

He rolled his eyes. "And I'm the one who doesn't

understand romance?"

He finally found Bella in the living room wedged between the sofa and an end table. He pulled some jerky from his pocket and, unable to resist her favorite treat, she tentatively approached him.

"I'm hoping to introduce my program at the Creative Technology Developer Conference in Vegas in a few months. It's starting a real buzz with new investors. Maybe you'll have your money back sooner than you think."

"Well, if that's the case, I'm a fan."

"Just say the word, and I can set you up with someone." She snapped her fingers to emphasize her point.

He held up both hands as if that would magically ward off any matchmaking thoughts that might be going through her head. "No thank you. I've realized I have the love of my life right here," he said, rubbing Bella's shaggy head. He doubted any match Kennedy could come up with would ever compare to Maddie, anyway.

"Fine. But my offer still stands. It's in my nature to help people."

"Then how about helping me get Bella in the bathtub?"

Kennedy looked down at his dog, and her eyes widened. Before she could answer, the doorbell sounded. Bella barked and made a beeline for the door.

She grinned. "Saved by the bell."

"Don't get too happy. You're not off the hook yet," he told her as he made his way to the door.

He grabbed Bella's collar and swung open the door.

And found the last person he'd ever expect on his front porch.

Trent blinked a few times to be sure. But it was Maddie,

completely lovely in a white sleeveless blouse and black flared skirt. Those crystal-blue eyes were locked on his. It hurt just to look at her.

"Hi," she said shyly.

"Maddie, I didn't expect to see you." He could barely keep his voice even.

Bella began to whine, wanting to get closer and check Maddie out. Maddie gazed down at his dog and raised her eyebrows. "Wow, you never mentioned that Bella was a lot of dog."

"And a lot of hair," he murmured, struggling to keep her from jumping up on Maddie.

Her gaze slowly traveled to him. "I suppose it is a lot of hair. But I like hairy dogs." A wide smile began to bloom from her mouth and she nodded. "Yeah, hairy is good. Real good."

"Um, okay…" He tried to sort through that "hairy" statement as Kennedy came up behind him.

"Trent, who is—" Her eyes widened. "Oh. Maddie. What are you doing here?"

Trent shot his cousin a look for asking the question before he could.

Maddie cleared her throat. "I came here to talk to Trent. Actually, to apologize to Trent."

Trent went completely still, hearing words that began to drop seeds of hope into his heart.

"Here, let me take Bella off your hands," his cousin said, taking Bella's collar and leading her out back. "I'll take her for a walk around the block a few times to give you some privacy."

"Yeah, thanks," he murmured, never taking his eyes off

Maddie.

Once they were alone, Maddie licked her lips. "May I come in?"

He blinked then took a step back. "Sorry."

Maddie walked in, rubbing her arms as if warding off a chill, but it was almost July, and the air conditioner wasn't turned on. It hadn't even been twenty-four hours, yet his eyes hungrily raked every inch of her. It was bliss to see her. Complete bliss and complete torture at the same time.

She glanced at him. Glanced away. Then glanced back and took a deep breath. "Trent, I'm crazy about you."

He stood there, amazed, shaken, and apparently mute, but very, very happy.

"I should have said this to you at the wedding, but I was afraid."

"That's okay, because you're telling me now. That's all that matters."

She closed the distance between them and gently reached up to run a finger down his jaw. "I'm glad it still matters to you."

"It does. After everything I went through with my botched engagement, it really does matter to me."

"You were right about me. I was so blinded by my own insecurities from being abandoned by my dad that I became my own curse."

"It's okay. We've both been abandoned. I know it's not easy to trust after something like that. But Maddie, I want you to trust me. So badly. Just know there are never any guarantees in life."

"I've done a lot of stupid things because of my fear of taking a chance on someone. But the most stupid thing I ever did was push you away."

He reached for her hand, held it tight. "I'm sure you've done stupider things."

She chuckled. "Like hire someone to attend my sister's wedding with me?"

"No, that was *not* stupid," he insisted. "Especially since it was me you hired."

"I'm glad you think that," she said, amusement lighting her eyes. "Because I was hoping you'd be available for one more job."

"Maddie, I told you. I'm not a paid escort."

"Oh, you aren't going to get paid. But I was wondering if you'd be available sometime to escort me on a date. A *real* date."

"Huh," he said, his lips curving into a smile. "A date with you? I guess I have to think about it."

"Since I hope to be working again soon, it would be my treat," she added.

"Okay, but just one date?"

She shrugged. "It's negotiable."

He pretended to think it over then tugged her into his arms, loving her softness and warmth. "I agree to your terms. And I just checked my schedule. Turns out I'm free."

"I was hoping you would be." She leaned forward and kissed him lightly on the lips, pulling back way too soon for his liking.

"So when do you want to go out?" she asked.

He smiled into her eyes. "I'm thinking every day this year."

Epilogue

"I thought we were going to stay in tonight."

Trent slid Maddie a mischievous side glance then put on his turn signal. He'd promised to cook for her at his place since she had the weekend off from her head pastry chef job at the Ritz Carlton. But he'd passed his house and had continued driving for the last fifteen minutes.

"You'll get your meal," he assured her. "I just have a little surprise for tonight's date night."

It was their one hundred and twentieth date night. But who was counting?

When she told him she'd given up believing she was cursed, she meant every word. The past several months with Trent had been anything but cursed. In fact, they'd been… perfect.

And speaking of perfect…

"Hey, I just got a save-the-date card in the mail. So Kennedy and Justin are really getting married?" she asked.

He nodded. "They sure are. Who knew true love could be manufactured by microchips?"

"I know people who've gotten together in stranger ways," she said with a grin.

He smiled. "Uh, true. They seem happy enough. Investors seem happy enough with her technology as well, because I got all my money back from her business plus a little something extra."

Maddie was thankful for that, because it meant Trent finally had the money to not only put into his gyms but also to add an addition for the youth program he wanted to start up.

The car finally slowed down. He pulled into the driveway of a fairly large coastal home with cedar shingles and a front yard full of lovely flowers in pinks, purples, and blues.

He parked the car and turned to her. "What do you think?"

She thought it was absolutely charming. "You're moving?" she said instead.

"Maybe." He gave her a hint of a smile then got out of the car. "Come on, let's take a peek inside."

Trent retrieved a key that was obviously left under the mat for him and opened the door. When she walked in, her breath caught at the shining hardwood floors and high cathedral-like ceilings. The kitchen and living room were large and open with plenty of windows to let in natural light and also showcase the view of the bay.

"My goodness, Trent. This is spectacular." She rushed over to the sliding back doors. "Oh, and look, there's plenty of space for Bella to run and play, too."

"Or children," he added, coming up behind her.

She turned and blinked twice at him, trying to keep her voice even. "Children?"

He slowly nodded. His eyes never leaving hers, he got down on one knee.

His hand reached for hers and held it tight. "Maddie, six months ago you hired me as your date to your sister's wedding. The best non-job I ever had, because I think I knew deep down in my heart almost from the beginning that I would always want you in my life. So now I'm asking you to be my wedding date. At *our* wedding."

The love reflected in his face made it a struggle to breathe. "Yes," she whispered.

"Thank God." He stood and fiercely hugged her to him. "I love you," he told her. "I love you so much—even though you still don't know what an onside kick is."

She laughed but a few tears slipped over her lashes. "Well, maybe not that. But I do know what a hot receiver is, because I happen to be engaged to one."

"Whew." He chuckled. "I guess we'll be okay then."

She kissed him, long and deep, until her head swam and, when she finally pulled back, she couldn't help grinning from ear to ear. "Yeah, I think we'll be just fine."

Acknowledgments

As per usual, BIG sloppy kisses to the women of my critique group: The Passionate Critters. In particular, I want to thank Keri, Julie, Bethanne, and Nina. I was on a deadline, and you ladies dropped everything to do some really fast reading. But I appreciate you ALL for the time, work, energy, empathy, advice, and laughs you give to me throughout the year.

More kisses to my husband and daughter who are extra supportive when I need to bounce ideas or need complete silence. I know I'm a pain sometimes.

No sloppy kisses (I'll spare you) but major THANKS and PRAISE to my favorite editor in the world, Stacy Cantor Abrams, and her partner in editing, Lydia Sharp. Thank you both for making this book so much stronger with your awesome suggestions and comments. You are both a joy to work with.

Lastly, thank you to the whole team at Entangled Publishing. I really am thrilled to have found such a wonderful publisher and am proud to be among so many talented authors.

About the Author

Jennifer Shirk has a bachelor's degree in pharmacy—which has in *no way* at all helped her with her writing career. But she likes to point it out, since it shows that romantic-at-hearts come in all shapes, sizes, and *mind-numbing* educations.

She writes sweet (and sometimes even funny) romances for Samhain Publishing, Montlake Romance, and Entangled Publishing. Recently, her novel *Sunny Days for Sam* won the 2013 Golden Quill Published Authors Contest for Best Traditional Romance.

Lately she's been on a serious exercise kick. But don't hold that against her. http://www.jennifershirk.com/

Also, if you liked this book, sign up for her newsletter and be the first to hear about her next release and a chance to win some awesome prizes: http://eepurl.com/Q6TH1

Discover the **Anyone But You** *series...*

Fiancé by Fate

Also by Jennifer Shirk

Kissing Kendall

A Little Bit Cupid

www.ingramcontent.com/pod-product-compliance
Lightning Source LLC
Chambersburg PA
CBHW020632180626
46816CB00003B/927